To the unheralded men of the 9th Defense Battalion of WWII and their successors, the 9th Antiaircraft Artillery Battalion. Here's thanks to you all, wherever you may be.

And to two sergeants: Dewey Brittain and Edmund Ferlas, consummate Marines. Without knowing them I could not have written this story.

Acknowledgments

My trials in becoming a writer have been many, and the growth in that direction could not have been accomplished without the help from my friends and family. First to my beloved Harriet who has put up with me these fifty years, and who at times set aside her own ambitions in the field of literature to guide me along. A word about my friend Joline Dorsan: she not only cleaned up my work, but also laid bare my characters' flaws. I wish to thank my good friend Jerry Maslon, whose knowledge of the Japanese helped me add credibility to the novel. Fellow veteran Vincent Quatro's enthusiasm for the novel, and the pride and gratitude he feels for the American fighting man, gave me reason to finish *Marines and Renegades*.

My new associates Dale and Julia Dye resurrected *Marines and Renegades*. After reading the novel, they felt it worth their time and abilities to publish. While Julia cleaned up the script grammatically, Dale added insight into the Marine fighting man's physique. While struggling with inept publishers, I lost sight of the significance of the novel. Dale and Julia's passion for *Marines and Renegades* reignited my need to bring the novel into the public eye. I thank you all.

Foreword

As a child of the World War II generation and a professional military man, I have an abiding interest in the most seminal world conflict of the 20th Century. I grew up listening to veterans' war stories from the ETO and the Pacific and I suppose that's where the fascination was engendered. When I enlisted in the Marine Corps I was force-fed large dollops of World War II history and my interest rapidly became a passion with an understandable emphasis on Marine campaigns in the Pacific. Over the intervening years I studied and even visited battle grounds on infamous islands such as Guadalcanal, Saipan, Guam, Peleliu, Iwo Jima and Okinawa.

My focus was on the brutal combat required to wrest these Pacific flyspecks from fanatical Japanese defenders until I ran across a book titled "No Surrender" by former Japanese soldier Hiroo Onoda who emerged from the Philippine jungle and gave himself up to allied authorities...in *March 1974*. Onoda was a renegade Japanese officer who refused to believe the war was really over despite evidence to the contrary and continued to evade and conduct a one-man guerilla campaign for thirty years after his nation surrendered. After a little research I discovered he wasn't the only Japanese hold-out in the Pacific; merely the longest post-war survivor on record. His revelations led me down an entirely different path in my studies of World War II and it was for the most part virgin territory.

Very little has been written about Japanese renegades on Pacific islands and even less about the American soldiers, sailors, airmen and Marines who occupied those hard-won islands after World War II ended. When that long, brutal and costly war ended in 1945, Americans were anxious to put it all behind and get on with peacetime pursuits. That's understandable but it leaves unplumbed a wealth of fascinating post-war stories that are both fascinating and revealing about men caught in the backwash of occupation duties. Those duties were particularly onerous and frustrating for men serving out their enlistments on Pacific islands like Guam in the Marianas that had both native populations and renegade Japanese soldiers. Those stories need to be told so we'll start right here with former Marine Gene Rackovitch's story *Marines and Renegades*.

Capt. Dale A. Dye, USMC (Ret.)

Introduction

The United States Marine Defense Battalions of World War II were a strange sort of combat command in the Corps' early wartime organization. They were neither purely dedicated coastal artillery units nor were they strictly antiaircraft artillery outfits, although they were manned and equipped to fight in both of those roles. Like many Marine Corps commands—such as Raider and parachute battalions—they were envisioned as performing specific, specialized missions but always expected to do whatever the situation demanded. And as war in the Pacific became bloodier and more chaotic, that most frequently meant serving as regular infantry or direct-support artillery.

There were twenty numbered Defense Battalions on the Corps' roles at the end of World War II, including two—the 51st and 52nd—that were composed of all black Marines commanded by white officers. Throughout the long campaigns that hopped from one bloody Pacific island to another, these Defense Battalions fought gamely and valiantly in whatever mission was assigned to them, often becoming just a spare infantry or fire-support command for whatever division they served. They were filled with yeomen of many military trades which made them very handy units from which hard-pressed commanders could cherry-pick critical skills on short notice and under extreme pressure.

In the original role for which they were first organized at the start of WWII, Marine Defense Battalions were sent to captured islands to guard against Japanese counterattack from the sea and to provide an antiaircraft umbrella over vital airfields. When an island was deemed safe from enemy counter-offensives, the assault force was redeployed and a defense battalion was left to guard the back-door and deal with Japanese hold-outs. Some 17,000 Marines served in defense battalions during the war and were deployed all across the Central and South Pacific. When the war ended, a good portion of the defense battalion commands were deactivated.

Those that remained were stuck on various islands throughout the Pacific. The complement was full of bored and often disgruntled men who either didn't have enough overseas points for rotation and discharge or those who reached the Pacific at the tail end of the fighting and still had a full enlistment to serve. They were leavened with career regulars. These Marines often became a de facto island garrison in which maintaining morale was often a bigger problem than dealing with Japanese stragglers and renegades who refused to surrender.

In the view of the Marine regulars, constant hard training was the best antidote to boredom but that led to monotony so many Marines volunteered for jungle patrols designed to ferret out Japanese stragglers. These patrols were usually mounted in response to complaints from islanders about renegades raiding their villages in search of food or other provisions. Going on one of these excursions could be dangerous as the Japanese soldiers there had lost none of their combat skills and were often in a desperate mind-set.

On Guam, where this story takes place, there were still hundreds of Japanese stragglers roaming the island's interior at war's end. Some Japanese soldiers held out for nearly 30 years after the surrender. Corporal Shoichi Yokoi was captured on Guam in January 1972. Although it can't be proven that he initiated any of the incidents described in this book, his rank made him senior to many of the other soldiers captured on Guam and his testimony provides some insight to events described in my story. My unit was the 9th Antiaircraft Battalion, originally the 9th Defense Battalion which had been re-designated in September 1944 when it was sent to the Marianas. While on Guam, I went on a number of these renegade-hunting patrols. The last one was mounted after four Marines were killed by the Japanese renegades. They had been combing Guam's hills for war souvenirs. Five went in and only one came out to report what happened at the hands of Japanese renegades. We did not find the culprits who killed the souvenir hunters. It was rare to encounter any of these Japanese soldiers; they had years of experience avoiding Marine patrols.

A few days later a contingent of U.S. Army airmen came into our camp. One of them spoke Japanese. He carried a bull horn and led a pair of former Japanese soldiers he'd managed to coax out of hiding in the jungles of Guam. As the former enemies bowed and smiled at us, I asked the interpreter if he thought they might have been in on the killing of our four Marine souvenir hunters. He avoided answering me and that has annoyed me ever since.

There has never been any justice for those Marines and many others military personnel plus a number of innocent Pacific islanders who were killed by Japanese renegades after the end of World War II. I thought then—as I think now—that someone should relate a thing or two about this unknown aspect of the Second World War's immediate aftermath. I give you *Marines and Renegades*.

Book 1

The Marines

Corporal Paul—September 1946

It was a difficult trek. The patrol was fruitless. They saw no one. The four Marines finally came to the crest of the second hill which put them closer to the sea. It was quiet there. Wisps of clouds passed overhead, threading across a rich blue sky. It was the highest point on Guam. At five hundred feet above sea level, storms washed the high ground but rarely descended to flush out the jungle below. A cool breeze blew over them. They rested.

The patrol was routine. Corporal Paul and three privates were sent out to see if they could find the Japanese renegades that stole a number of hams and a sack of dried corn from one of the outlying villages. It wasn't the stealing that disturbed the villagers; it was the appearance of the renegades that was unsettling. The Japs were seen running from the village, sticks for legs and arms, joints bulging from emaciated bodies. One turned just before they disappeared into the surrounding jungle, A weird smile—half glee and half relief—crossed the renegade's face when he realized they were not pursued. He hopped up and down as he disappeared into the tall grass surrounding the village.

They did not have to cover much ground. They were ordered to cross two of the highest ridges, go into the jungle, search around a bit, then retrace their steps back to the sea where a truck waited to pick them up. The first half of their route complete, the Marines cracked their canteens and drank. Cartridge belts and weapons were stacked in the center of a small depression on the top of the hill. They could hear the surf breaking on the beach below; a swishing sound reached them as the breakers freed sand. The outgoing sea resettled the grains. The sound reminded Corporal Paul of the new jetty built by the Seabees that subdued the surf and gave the military personnel remaining on Guam a place to enjoy the sun and sea.

Yeah, thought Paul, *they have floats down there...ya can swim out to them. The water is clear as glass, cool and clean.*

He knew his patrol should comb the slope leading to the sea, form a skirmish line and sweep to the beach, but he figured a little rest wouldn't hurt and there was plenty of time to complete their mission.

~~~~~~~~~~~~~~~

They waited until they saw no further movement from the four Marines on the hill and then the three renegades moved out, each taking a different path up the hill to its crest. Their footsteps were so sure, not a stone was overturned, not a pebble brushed out of place to sound an alarm. Animal existence brought archaic senses to life more than the most rigorous training, or the traditions of the Samurai, the great warriors of Imperial Japan. All that was nothing compared to skills honed in months of hiding from the Americans after they recaptured Guam. The quick runs through the jungle, sitting motionless for hours, sometimes days, until danger passed: those were the skills that kept the renegades alive. They spent their days slithering through a maze of jungle, realizing any encounter with Americans could be their last. The renegades lived by primitive rules and animal instincts tempered by daring, fear and intuition.

Their lives were far removed from life in the cities, rice paddies, and parade grounds of Japan. Starvation was their constant companion on Guam. Fresh meat taken from native village was a luxury; going without food would not be an option anymore. They would be more brazen from now on to satisfy their needs. Their cache of spare weapons and ammunition had been discovered by previous patrols. Their remaining cartridges would be used in this engagement. Normally, they prayed prior to a mission but that semblance of routine was now abandoned. The death of the Marines would mean nothing. The renegades were marking time until the Imperial Japanese Army came to retake the island. They were still soldiers and the mission they planned would reinforce their credo. With the weapons they wished to take from the Marines their situation would be improved. The Marines slept.

The Marines knew it was very important to have clean weapons; theirs were spotless. Ironically, they were stacked out of reach.

The Japanese soldiers eased their way to the crest. When each man was in position with his weapons ready, the leader pointed out a Marine target for each of his men. With targets designated, each renegade Japanese soldier carefully aimed his weapon at one of the sleeping Marines. At his signal they fired.

~~~~~~~~~~~~~~~

A thud, pressure on the brain, a flash of intense light, then peace before they died. None of them heard a sound except for Cpl. Paul who now faced a wall of muzzles trained on him. Paul made a motion, a last effort to avoid disaster. His shoulder twitched forward, arm extended, as reflexes honed in solid military training planed to perpetuate *esprit de corps* were negated by a mistake. A thoughtless move set aside the efforts combat coordinators, field generals and sergeants beleaguered by training manuals. He'd made a fatal mistake. He'd ignored a basic principle of ground combat familiar to all soldiers. *The guard*, Paul thought. *I didn't post a guard.*

He eyed the bayonet attached to his cartridge belt but it was out of reach. His eyes flicked toward the edge of the crest.

Maybe over the side, no, dead, you'll be dead! Too far, too far....

The renegade leader picked up an M-1 rifle and put one round into Paul's body. *Good rifle, Garand. Keep it clean, it hardly ever misfires, works like a charm.* Paul remembered that as he pondered the slug that tore through his chest. He became angry at what he had done. He'd killed his men as sure as the Japanese renegades. He'd screwed up the mission by failing to post a guard. It was such a simple thing and such a mortal sin, a sin. He felt he should die for that indiscretion alone, for his stupidity.

Home, home, Chicago; crisp, clean, cold, winter Chicago; bitter cold Chicago; dirty Chicago. Mother at the old coal stove in the linoleum-covered flat, four flights up, old doors, old house. Tired old lady, Mother should not be that old.

Pretty girl from the other side of town, talked all the time, liked the way he dressed, the way he looked at her excited her. She wanted to grab hold of him and press him to her without reservation.

"Oh, God...God!" Paul shouted. He made one last defiant act by spitting at the Japanese soldiers. It was as much a display of anger at his own failure as it was rage against the men standing over him. A stream of blood spewed from his mouth and dribbled down the front of his dungaree shirt. The renegade leader pulled the trigger again and put a second round into Cpl. Paul.

He stared dispassionately at the man he'd just shot, thinking about the efficient action of the American rifle. He spent a few moments like a well-trained soldier pondering the functionality of the weapon and how well it was designed. Then he reverted to the primitive and reached for one of the captured American bayonets.

~~~~~~~~~~~~~~~

"Chicaga, Chicaga," the Negro boy said to Paul as they walked to school.
"It's not Chicaga, it's Chicago, Chicago."

Paul could not understand why that incident came into his mind just then as a bluish light settled on him, turned purple, then black, darker, and darker. Out of the darkness the girl with bright, beautiful teeth smiled at him.

~~~~~~~~~~~~~~~

The renegades plunged a captured bayonet into each Marine. The leader admired the keen edge on the blade. It was Paul's. Paul thought it important to keep the blade sharp. The renegade leader also believed it very important to keep all edged weapons razor-sharp. He used the sharp edge of Cpl. Paul's bayonet to cut the patrol leader's throat. It really wasn't necessary. There was no heartbeat and no blood gushed from the gaping wound.

~~~~~~~~~~~~~~~

The driver of the ten-wheel, two-and-a-half ton Marine Corps truck lay back on his seat, his head resting on the door of the truck. His Marine dungaree cap was pulled down over his eyes. He waited. A breeze from the sea brushed his face. He sat up and checked his watch. *They should have been here by now,* he thought. He fidgeted. Bored, he toyed with his watch, a beautiful Swiss watch that cost him six dollars at the PX. He never saw anything like it in Alabama. It had a stop-watch function and he marveled at the fluorescent hands; he could see them clearly at night. He thought of the farm and the huge alarm clock in his room back home. The thunder of it as it woke him, splitting the silence of the country air. The blackness outside, the fringe of light slicing the horizon; he pulled the down cover over his head every morning. Three hours he waited for the patrol to appear.

Should I go into the jungle and look for them? No, he decided, *I gotta watch the truck.*

He had to wait, had to stay with the truck and little else mattered. The Marines gave him a truck to drive; that gave him status, something a farm boy from Alabama needed when it came to dealing with the city boys that seemed to be everywhere in the 9th Antiaircraft Battalion on Guam. He had his pride wrapped up in this greasy old mud-spattered truck. He climbed out of the cab and walked around the vehicle, marveled at it: a machine and it was his. He kicked at the sand on the shoulder of the road and remembered how the government came to Alabama and built roads.

Roads, the government always builds roads. When the government goes somewhere they build roads, real concrete roads. The government built a road ta home there's a lota folks passin' by all the time now.

He turned his thoughts to the patrol. *Damn Yankees...that snot-ass Corporal Paul from Chicago...like to shove a stump up that Yankee's ass.* The Alabama boy stood a foot taller than Paul but a corporal was an NCO and had authority. He learned about that early in his time in the Marine Corps after serving 21 days in the brig on bread and water for challenging the authority of his CO. Anybody with a stripe on his sleeve or a bar on his collar could put him in the brig again and he'd had all he needed of that. So he waited and hoped he was doing the right thing.

~~~~~~~~~~~~~~~

The Japanese renegades stripped the bodies of all their clothing and equipment and then arranged the corpses in a single line abreast. The leader didn't believe in mutilation. He believed in spirits, and that cutting up the bodies would leave spirits in limbo. Leaving the bodies whole might also keep them from being mutilated if they were eventually captured. It had been a long time since the main battle in the grove where they were overrun during the initial fighting for Guam and the Americans had only come after them in force once. That happened immediately after his soldiers had killed two of three unarmed Marines.

Those Americans were stupid. They didn't bother to take weapons along in the jungle, remembered the senior renegade.

One Marine escaped and that's when the intense hounding began. Many patrols scoured the area; they were not discovered.

The renegades slipped off the hill, crouching low as they disappeared silently into the bush. They moved quietly, quieter than the crawling insects and creatures there. Sound did not carry far in the humid air surrounding the underbrush...yet they had learned not to be careless.

~~~~~~~~~~~~~~~

A Jeep carrying a lieutenant and a private pulled up beside the truck. The lieutenant dismounted and spoke to the driver from Alabama. He wanted to know why he hadn't returned to base and reported the overdue patrol. It was the lieutenant's patrol that was missing and it was his responsibility to find out what had become of them. That was fairly normal except for the fact that the officer had sent out this patrol without reporting it to his parent command; it was unauthorized.

Eventually, the lieutenant would have to face his colonel and try to explain why he ignored the chain of command and sent out an unauthorized patrol. If something bad happened to the four Marines, he was in trouble. Chewing out the befuddled driver seemed to help a little, just to ease his own insecurity in the matter.

He should never have allowed his company office clerks to conduct the patrol without assigning one of the old salts from his command. They were anxious volunteers, that wouldn't help when he had to face the music. And those old line sergeants had just sneered at him when he asked for a veteran to lead the patrol. They wanted nothing to do with boot officers and he had a corporal in charge. Let the man do his job for once and lead a three-man patrol; that was their advice.

The lieutenant knew a patrol of this sort should have been turned over to the island Military Police. It seemed so simple; any trained Marine outfit should be able to handle it with no problem. Cpl. Paul was capable, wasn't he?

They're all Marines, he rationalized. *All combat trained; it's a minor thing, a patrol.*

I'd better get moving. Christ, I've waited too long already. That red faced Colonel is going to make me feel like shit. Should have known better, should have reported it sooner. It's done now. Better get the hell back and deal with it. Maybe they're just lost up in the hills somewhere.

Gunnery Sergeant Killian

The military police were sent out; they found the bodies. Gunnery Sergeant Killian was in charge of bringing them out. He was angry.

"Come on; get the stupid bastards off this hill. Dumb fucks let the Japs take their weapons. Marines...bullshit! Damn yard birds!"

The working party, all recent replacements, were stunned at the Gunny's rage but they knew enough not to confront him with their feelings.

"What the fuck ya lookin' at? Just get 'em outta here. Ya want to see a stupid bunch of Marines? There they are right in front of ya, letting them assholes get the best of them! They had to be sleepin'. No guard! That should teach ya something. Get 'em outta here! And don't give me them dirty looks. Just do it."

The working party of Marines increased their efforts and did not look again at the sergeant. Killian watched as they put Paul's body on a stretcher. He remembered the corporal: *I know that Paul. He should have had more sense. If they were ambushed, I could understand, but getting caught this way is a goddamn shame. Look at 'em. Stiff as boards! These boys are gonna sweat getting them down to the trucks. Never know about people. Thought Paul had more brains. Marines...shit!*

There was no questioning the Gunny. He was 42 years old and a renowned veteran of the Banana Fleet Marines. He was one of those old gnarled jarheads that served with the Corps in the Mosquito Coast for decades, honing their combat skills in the jungles of Central America. Most made way for the Gunny. He stood raw-boned at six foot two with a depression-rendered lean body. There was a perpetual sneer on his face that only softened after the consumption of huge amounts rye whiskey.

Killian was on Saipan with the 4th Marine Division where he established an exemplary combat record. He was held in awe by veterans and subordinates alike. The Gunny feared no one. His command of creative profanity was renowned throughout the unit. He used it on everyone—officers or enlisted men—when they were doing something stupid.

Many of the Marines who demonstrated exceptional gallantry on Saipan were offered battlefield commissions. Gunny Killian was one of them. His regimental commander thought he was too old and refused Killian's recommendation. The Company Commander passed the word and promptly got a typical reaction from the sergeant to take back to the colonel. "You tell that fucking turd that if I'm too old to be an officer then I'm too old to fight for him. I'm goin' home."

There was no argument. Gunny Killian was sent home.

One year in the states re-ignited a wanderlust that haunted him since the first time he jumped a freight train during the depression. He requested orders for an overseas assignment. The post commander simply shook his head, and handed the Gunny his orders. His new port of call was Guam.

In Hungarian culture, the surname takes precedence. Corporal Drago Stoyon was christened Hugarie Dragomier Stoyonovitch. It was Hunky from his father, Croat from his mother, and Serb from his grandfather. Drago rebelled against Old World patriarchy and altered the name on his birth certificate to read Drago Stoyon.

As the patrol assembled, Cpl. Drago Stoyon thought that things were starting off badly. They were supposed to leave at 0800 and they hadn't moved until an hour later. Charlie Conjolies, the Italian from Brooklyn, started horsing around with a grenade. He pulled the pin and then couldn't get it re-seated. That involved a trip to the Quartermaster Sergeant who couldn't get the pin back in the grenade, either. He just bound the safety lever with tape and sent Conjolies on his way with an ass-chewing. The QM sergeant would dispose of the grenade later in the day by tossing it into the water off the beach. It was a good way to stun fish and usually provided a tasty alternative to mess hall fare on Guam.

Charles Conjolies made it back in time to board the truck. They were finally on their way.

Good trucks, thought Drago. *Corps made a good choice goin' with the big Internationals. The corporal in charge of the motor pool don't know squat. Still they put him in charge. Happens like that sometimes.*

Most of the veteran sergeants in Drago's outfit were rotated home after the war ended. That left junior non-commissioned officers in charge in certain situations.

Some good, some bad, thought Drago. *This Corporal Marino they got running the motor pool, he's from Long*

Island. He's got brothers in the trucking business. They must have all the brains 'cause this guy is missin' a couple of nuts and bolts.

Stoyon watched the motor pool corporal. Every once in a while he caught him off guard and saw a look of confusion on his face. At home, Marino's brothers showed no mercy. Following a boot in the ass or a cuff on the side of the head, they took over any job the younger Marino botched. It was no different in the Marine Corps; there was always someone more competent to take over when Marino screwed things up. In this outfit it was Private Migilano, an expert mechanic, green as new corn and right out of Sicily. Migilano was glad to take over for the inept corporal. Migliano wished to please; Marino sought him out to cover his own incompetence. Drago Stoyon was wise to Marino.

The truck was loaded and put in gear.

Stoyon rode in the back of the truck next to Fat Tom and Charlie Conjolies. The incident with the grenade and a decision to issue Conjolies a Thompson sub-machine-gun had Stoyon worried. The Guinea had no idea how to use the weapon. When Stoyon quizzed him about it, Conjolies couldn't answer any of the pertinent questions. Fat Tom was familiar with the Thompson, so Stoyon had him instruct Conjolies before they departed. Still, he didn't like the situation and felt uneasy about the patrol.

Two guys with Thompson machine guns—one don't know how to use it—on a patrol hunting renegades, Drago thought. And that live grenade deal...better be careful. This could turn out shitty.

As Stoyon mulled over the situation, things got worse. Cpl. Marino drove the six-by-six up the wrong road which narrowed as they went uphill. The truck was quickly hemmed in by trees and vegetation. Sharp blades of grass and tree limbs swatted the Marines riding in the back of the vehicle. They all left the comfort of the bench seats and huddled in the well of the cargo bay. That was not the end of it. Before the motor pool corporal decided to back down the trail, they ran into a nest of spiders. Their webs in the trees created a canopy across the road. Little red spiders—hundreds of them— crawled all over the Marines in the cab and in the back of the truck. The Marines tried to brush them off. They were swatting, cursing, spitting and knocking each other down in an effort to dislodge them. That sent the spiders into a frenzy to avoid the swatting hands. Some of the Marines looked frightened, some annoyed, but most were angry at the skittering swarm, at the stupid motor pool corporal, at the swatting, stinging branches.

"Fer Christ sakes; what's that stupid bastard doin' now?" blurted Drago as the truck halted.

Gears clanged, the transmission groaned as the truck was jammed into reverse. They went down the hill backwards; the motor pool corporal's head out of the window, peering, squinting, as he guided the truck down the trail. They went back through the spider webs and the Marines prepared for another encounter with the darting pests.

Bastards. Don't like to squash 'em, Drago thought. *They spread watery when ya smash 'em. Ya get that yellow ooze all over....*

But the spiders had dispersed into the foliage, to suck the life of their victims away from the roving of man, and the stupidity of motor pool corporals.

Drago and the Pepper

Corporal Stoyon was annoyed. A minute ago he was dry, now water was pouring from his body. His dungarees were dry only in spots where they didn't touch his skin. It wasn't that he did not know what sweat was, but this was different. As he entered the jungle he could feel the change in his body. It was hot but not hot enough to warrant the amount of perspiration pumping out of his pores. The foliage was thick off the trail. Soft palms vined to suffocation, their fronds rising above the forest floor to let the trunks suffer the indignity of the oppressive humidity.

~~~~~~~~~~~~~~~

The jungle humidity was different from the heat of the mills in Steeltown. It was Steeltown to the bankers and teachers, Schtellton to the Croats and Germans who worked in the mills. The heat of the jungle was not as intense as the ingots coming out of the mill furnaces. That was a burning, searing heat. Drago knew that heat. The fire in the open hearth at the mill drew him, making him stand absorbing the heat longer than he should have. It was familiar to him. The humidity in the jungle was different. It agitated Drago.

Drago decided to work in the mill. The money was better than working at the bank, his first job after leaving high school. He would soon be in the service and wanted the extra money the mill job offered to raise a little hell before committing to the military.

Only once before had he perspired like he did now. It was at the dinner table; the hot pepper. He thought of that night and his father—the Hunky, they called him in the predominantly Slavic neighborhood. His father was born in Hungary, in a town north of the Danube where he met Drago's mother. She was the child of a Croatian mother and Serbian father. Hundreds of years of diverse nationalism and variances in religious persuasion did not accept the union; yet they survived. His father an immense man: square-jawed, thick-lipped, with pock-marked cheeks; he sported a wrinkled brow for as long as Drago could remember. A handlebar moustache covered a full upper lip without which his face would have looked foolish. It was stained yellow at the tips from perpetual twisting of chewing-tobacco-stained fingers.

But the peppers; the family seated at the dinner table. Drago sat at the dinner table in the second seat to the left of his father. His three older brothers were seated by age on the left and right of the patriarch. His six sisters, all younger than Drago, were seated also by age farther down. His mother was seated at the end of the table, near the kitchen, placed there for instantaneous response to any command from the old Hungarian grenadier.

Drago's father, a grenadier sergeant, held a position as senior non-commissioned officer, which was subverted by the voluminous desertions of the Serbian irregulars under his command on the Russian front. These desertions caused a major defeat of the great Austrian Hungarian Army. He was flogged and disgraced by the incident. "They deserted not to fight again," he told his wife, "but for sanctions alone. I have not had the honor of killing any of the scum."

"Drago, my boy, my Croat..." The old man said as he spread his gnarled fingers on the table top. "You will try the pepper tonight; yes, Drago?" Bright blue eyes under shaggy brows challenged Drago. It was his turn. His brothers had already been tested; they fared well enough. Drago knew the ritual would be different for him. His father would save the hottest, reddest pepper for his youngest son. Only a pepper hot enough to make the old man smart would be for him.

Drago, the dark-haired, olive-skinned Croat. He was different than his brothers. They resembled the fair-haired Maygar of old; they were square-jawed with six-foot frames, going to one hundred eighty pounds, broad of chest and muscled to Barbarian proportions. Drago was the opposite, dark and relatively short at five-foot-seven, not going over one hundred thirty pounds. The only resemblance to the Hungarian in Drago was his piercing blue eyes inherited from his father.

His Hunky brothers had nothing on Drago on the football field. They were clumsy while he was quick and lithe. He could take out a boy weighing 200 pounds or better with no trouble. He learned to tumble early to avoid absorbing the full force of any contact. He knew when to go limp to avoid being crushed under their falling weight. He could get into the opposing backfield fast, spinning through defending guards and tackles. A slap on the side of the head of an aggressive lineman left a gap for the Croat to intrude and disrupt the opposition's play. Perplexed looks on their faces turned to anger as they realized the play was doomed. It amused Drago. He had talent; he was also hot-headed. When he called his coach an asshole for pulling him out of a game, he was kicked off the football team. Drago quit school that semester. Football was the only reason he stayed in school.

Football was his passion; without being allowed to play there was no need for him to stay in school. Study and social activity did not interest him. He loved a challenge;

he faced a big one at the dinner table that night. The pepper.

"Would you like to try the pepper?" The old man reached for the scorching vegetable as the others around the table snickered. "It is sweet, Drago." The grenadier's pursed lips mocked the boy.

His father's hand engulfed the red pepper as he held the fire toward his son. Drago snatched it from his father and took a big bite. The heat from the seeds in the husk burned past the layers of the outer pepper to enflame the roof, the teeth and the tongue. Drago's entire mouth was on fire. His cheeks turned red; the flame singed his throat. Sweat glistened all over his face. Drago didn't chew; he swallowed. When the fire reached his stomach, it sent a message to his nerves, which sent his entire system into overdrive fighting the flames.

"Water, my boy?" His father picked up a glass of water and held it out to him. Drago's fist flew striking the glass; it smashed on the wall behind his father. The water stained the wall. The liquid Drago needed to put the flame to rest dripped slowly down the wall, darkening on its decent. He was transfixed watching it. The heat of the pepper ignited a hatred toward the old grenadier. Drago turned to face his father, glaring, clenched teeth grinding, partly to quell, partly in anger at the old man.

His father stiffened. All was quiet at the table. His father's hands pressed down on the table top causing it to lift slightly on the opposite end. His mother sighed. She spread her fingers above the table top; moving them back and forth in a brushing motion, she thought her action could stem the disaster she believed was about to occur. His father's hands relaxed. The stern expression softened. He laughed.

"My little Croat has a temper," he laughed. "Oh God, the fire is in him! Look at my little Croat." Drago wanted to laugh, too, for his father never laughed. He'd won the contest. He wanted to laugh; to shout for joy.

The Hungarian knew that his son would not again be put upon, so he laughed to hide his secret delight. He had a son in this one, a real son. None of the others had shot back at him, only this little boy, the little Croat.

Drago didn't laugh; the fire was still burning. All through the meal he drank no water. He finished his supper and asked to be excused. Then he went down the street to a friend's house that had a pump in the backyard. He pumped water; letting it sluice into his mouth, trying to douse the fire. He put his head under the flowing water and let the cooling power of it engulf him. He held it there for many minutes, showering himself with the water and forcing it into his mouth in huge gulps.

Then he stopped pumping and headed for the railroad tracks behind the house. He sat on the silvery traversed rails; he fussed with the acid earth darkened by the soot from the mill, moving his foot back and forth in the grime. He fumed, biting his lip to hold back the welling tears. The pepper still burned.

The Bulletin

That was the last time Drago had sweated so profusely. The recollection sent a shiver through his body. He ran his thumb across his forehead, spraying sweat into the foliage. The Corps and the patrol intruded on his thoughts as he brushed aside tall jungle grass while moving forward. Mike Radackovitch came to mind, the tall Serb from Paterson, New Jersey. Mike worked in a ship yard as a burner, molding portholes in ship hulls. Mike was tall and slender, long-chinned...looking more German than Serbian.

Germans don't smile much, thought Drago. Mike was always smiling, grinning and laughing. Serbs smiled a lot. Croats didn't drink with Serbs. It was something about serfdom under the Serbian king. But Drago drank with them, went to their church hall, drank and laughed with them. Drago remembered that Mike got cut in a fight while in the Civilian Conservation Corps. He lost two-thirds of his intestines in that fight...but he still smiled. *For a guy with no guts left*, Drago mused, *he sure could put away the booze, take a hooker, drop it into a glass of beer, tip it and knock it off in one swallow.*

"The C's is just like the Army," Mike once told Drago. "Ya have ta remember this: 'yes sir, no sir, and no excuse sir'. Don't open yer mouth fer nothin' else. Most of all never volunteer fer nothin'."

I did fine with that up to now, Drago thought. *Then I had to read that freakin' bulletin board. Passed it a hundred times, never even noticed it. Just had to stop that day and take a look at that impressive piece of paper.*

Fleet Marine Forces—Pacific
Marianas Command Bulletin
12 September 1946

From : Commanding General
To :   CO,   9th   Antiaircraft   Artillery
Battalion

Subj : Japanese Forces remaining on
Guam, disposition of

1. The Commanding Officer is herewith
directed to organize regular patrols into the
island interior with the mission of seeking
out renegade Japanese who are creating
unrest among the civilian populations on
Guam.

2. Patrol activity will commence on 15
September 1946.

3. Patrols will be composed of no fewer than
sixteen (16) infantry-trained Marines led by
a commissioned officer.

4. It is desired that all USMC personnel
participating in these patrols be volunteers.

Thomas Simpson
Brig. Gen. USMCI

Oh, yeah, Drago thought as he pushed forward
streaming sweat and trying to keep an eye on his fellow
volunteers. *Ya see a movie like Guadalcanal Diary, ya join*

the fuckin' Marines. See a bulletin, join a patrol. Situations of unrest, my ass! They killed four shit-birds parked up on a hill takin' a snooze. Great. Here you are, haven't got enough brains not to volunteer. Oh yeah, a commissioned officer? A chicken shit second louie is what we got.

Perlas

Drago passed Sgt. Perlas on his way to the sergeant major's office. Earlier, they had discussed the possibility of Drago volunteering for the patrol.

"Hey, Stoyon! Ya gonna sign up?" Perlas cried out.

Perlas was standing some distance from Drago. He made no move to come closer, just clenched his fist with a thumb pointed to the sky. As Drago watched, the sergeant turned his wrist and brought the thumb down pointing to the ground. He stood there mocking, grinning, waiting for a reply.

"Screw you, Perlas." Drago raised his middle finger toward the heavens. He liked Platoon Sergeant Perlas, who was more intellectual than most. Perlas had enlisted as a grunt which had perplexed his friends and family. They pictured him an officer. He was burly, thick-bodied and tough with a round, pock-marked face. There was no nonsense about Perlas; he was proud to be a Marine. He'd fought through Guadalcanal and most of the Pacific campaigns before landing a post-war billet on Guam.

Perlas knew he was blessed being in an antiaircraft unit throughout the war. Although service in a Defense Battalion was hairy at times, it was nothing compared to foot slogging in the infantry.

While in New Georgia, it was the first but not the last time his unit was called upon to use their infantry training. The Army's 25th Division there was taking a beating from a superior Japanese force. The Army units were split leaving a gap that put the whole army in jeopardy. They were called on to close the gap; they held the imperial forces in check until the army was able to fill it. On leaving, the

Marines took their wounded and their dead out. They passed the soldiers they were replacing. Perlas was in the lead; he turned to the men following and shouted out, "Smarten up." The Marines understood, closed ranks and marched out...chins held high, smiling. They were awarded a Presidential Unit Citation for their action; from the President, not the Army. The Army saved their praise for their own.

After New Georgia, Perlas was sent back to the states for schooling. That gave him a full six months out of combat. Moving through Apra Harbor on his return to Guam, the destroyer escort he was aboard had to weave through skeletons of ships buried deep, their masts protruding above the water as they maneuvered to the docks. Perlas realized how luck played its hand in his favor. At the end of the war, Guam was a now safe haven for him.

While he was stateside, he met his future wife. She was engaged to a Marine second lieutenant at the base where Perlas was stationed. Perlas became so taken with her he approached her one day promising her a great life with a good man. At first she was stunned, and then insulted that this brash NCO had the nerve to propose anything to her, much less marriage. Soon enough the look of astonishment left her face. She laughed, then smiled at this daring man, and said she would think it over. That was good enough for Perlas, who promised to write often. They'd get to know each other better and get married as soon as he finished his tour on Guam.

That was Perlas. Small in stature for an NCO in a world where big men seemed to dominate, his mind was so quick he was rarely denied what he went after. Built hard as a rock short and stocky, Stoyon once heard another Marine say cannon balls would bounce off Perlas.

Perlas thought well of Cpl. Drago Stoyon. There were times when they were able to save each other embarrassment or reprimand from the brass.

Callahan

On Guam at that time, there was always the problem of Japanese renegades infiltrating. To insure that there were no problems, each man posted had to report to the guard house upon completion of his rounds, and sign a ledger. One evening when Stoyon was corporal of the guard and Perlas was the sergeant in charge, Perlas checked the ledger and realized one of the men had not signed three times in succession.

Perlas confronted Drago. They both understood that after the first time his negligence should have been reported to the standing officer of the day.

That meant trouble with Lt. Cantone, the Officer of the Day and a ball buster, and a man neither Perlas nor Drago could tolerate. Perlas reminded Stoyon that Cantone would have both of their stripes for spitting if he could; no less for their carelessness. They were in deep shit unless something was done about the log in a hurry.

Perlas stayed in the guard shack to fend off inquiries by the Commander of the Guard while Drago took off to locate the sentry. The renegades were still active, though it was improbable they would cause any trouble this far out of the jungle. Vegetation was sparse, leaving the renegades less cover in which to hide.

Drago carried a .45 pistol on his hip but that didn't provide much comfort.

Of all the things to carry, he thought. *I hate this piece of shit. I can't hit nothin' with it, and don't know who can. If I get in trouble I'm totally lost. It's useless. And if they've taken Callahan's rifle away from him, they'll damn sure use it on me.*

With his senses on full alert, Drago scoured the sentry's designated patrol route. He went around the Quartermaster's area, through the motor pool, past sick bay and then back to the guard shack.

Private Callahan was the lost sentry; he was nowhere to be found. Drago knew the man to be a mental fuck-up; one of the draftees taken into the Corps toward the end of the war. Most adapted well but many others constantly bitched and demeaned the Marine Corps. Callahan was one of those malcontents. He kept to himself, alternating between being surly and skirting any task put to him. He was a loner. Callahan had no friends.

Desperate at this point, Drago retraced his steps and made another tour of the sentry's patrol route. He was nearing the guard shack when he heard a noise from somewhere between the two Quonset huts of the sick bay. He pulled his pistol from its holster. He stopped to listen. He could not place the sound he heard; a rasping, gasping noise, strange, but yet familiar.

That's snoring! Drago recognized the sound as he got closer. *Someone is snoring! That fucker is asleep on post! That goddamn fool is asleep on watch!*

Callahan was asleep on one of the benches used by Marines waiting to be admitted for sick-call. All the pent up adrenaline-fueled anger in Drago burst out. He snatched Callahan up and began to pound him against the Quonset wall. The sleeping Callahan embraced his rifle with his two arms. As the corporal pounded him against the wall, to his merit or from just plain good training, he held on to the weapon.

"You asshole! You're sleepin' on my post, you rat bastard. I should just shoot your ass, you lousy prick!"

The fear in the eyes of Pvt. Callahan would remain with him for the rest of his life. What passed through his mind when the corporal grabbed him he could not remember, but then and there death presented itself.

The corporal's stature was on a par with that of the private, yet when he threw him into the road, the private's feet did not touch the ground until he was in the middle of the thoroughfare.

Drago was on him again.

"Move, you fucker! Move, you fucker, or I'll kick the shit out of you some more! Sleep on my post, will ya!"

Drago's thoughts swirled as he tried to control his rage. *Coulda cost me my stripes. Coulda fucked all over Perlas and me both. I want these stripes. I worked hard for 'em. An asshole like this ain't gonna get them taken away from me.*

Callahan was just standing in the road, shocked and scared. Drago shoved him toward the guard shack. "Get yer ass movin', ya fuckin' yardbird!" When Callahan failed to respond, Drago kicked him in the ass. "Move, you son of a bitch!" Drago kicked him again. Callahan finally started to move.

Of all the tenants of the Corps, the responsibilities of a sentry on post impressed him most. Sleeping on guard could get Marines killed. It could change the outcome of a battle. But it could also cost Perlas and Drago their rank, which was more important at this point.

He booted Pvt. Callahan into the guard shack and pointed at the logbook. "Sign your name in the open spaces in the ledger. Sign it four times, ya fuck-up. Get it done now!"

Callahan took the pencil off the desk and quickly signed. When he was finished, Callahan noted Stoyon's fists were still clenched and he shifted closer to the desk where there was not enough room for the corporal to aim another kick. Drago jerked a thumb toward the door.

"You're relieved, ya prick! Consider yourself lucky that it's only me and Perlas here or your ass would be on the way to Portsmouth." The mention of the infamous U.S. Naval Disciplinary Barracks at Portsmouth, New Hampshire put the fear of God into many Marines but it didn't seem to faze Callahan. Drago was about to add further instructions when he noticed Perlas standing nearby with a relief sentry to replace Callahan.

"I see you found him," said Perlas. He'd been watching the episode play out before posting the relief.

"Yeah, I found the prick."

Platoon Sergeant Perlas walked off to post the new sentry, carefully putting the incident in a mental file he kept on all junior NCOs. He and Braxton had been trying to make up their minds about who to recommend for the sergeant's test they were putting together. He'd put Cpl. Stoyon's name up for consideration twice before, and he was about to do it for a third time. He would sit down with Braxton after chow and discuss it further.

The Excursion

Drago's actions on an excursion outside the base finally convinced the sergeants he was worth consideration for a third stripe. It was a little off-duty trip to an outlying village that turned into a disaster. The escapade started when Cpl. Flint approached PlSgt. Braxton, bitching.

"I've been here six months now," Cpl. Flint said. "And if I don't get out and get some booze and a little pussy I think I'm gonna go nuts and something real bad is gonna happen."

Braxton knew Flint's reputation. The man had seven Private First Class Warrants stuffed in his locker. He was the oldest corporal in the outfit at 27 and a veteran of the 3rd Marines, who were given the unique charge of protecting the people of Iceland from the Germans. The salt in his veins spilled over into a brashness that amused the sergeants, but deserved consideration.

When the plan finally came together, Flint, Stoyon, and Cpl. Juarez were selected to go on the outing. Sgt. Perlas would drive them in a Jeep commandeered from the motor pool. He knew the way to their destination. They would go into a remote village for steak dinners and whatever else was available. The fact that all local villages on Guam were strictly off-limits didn't enter into the plan. Neither did the nightsticks of the roving MPs that controlled access to the villages. This was to be an exclusive deal, not like the command-sponsored dances that were held in Agana every six months or so. With over a thousand Marines on Guam, it was at least a hundred to one shot to get a dance with a local woman much less anything else, and as Cpl. Flint said, "I'd rather beat my meat than try to make out with those ugly Chamorro girls." The hamlet they had in mind was a little settlement that Sgt. Braxton knew about from a blonde nurse at the Naval Hospital in Agana. She'd introduced him to a nice little secluded restaurant in the village where steak dinners were available. The blonde who was his companion one evening was one of those lucky breaks in life. His time in combat included many instances where luck took over. He was outside their base walking down a road to the Seabees stationed just up the hill from them when a Jeep with the nurse driving down the road stopped and asked if he needed a lift. Luck, he smiled, and said "yes."

Nurses and USO matrons were not to be shared. Mint brandy and other intoxicants not palatable for senior NCOs were available to the corporals. The Canadian Club, Wild Turkey and Scotch the sergeants shared with the Seabees on the tugs in Apra Harbor were under lock and key.

They headed for the village that Saturday night. Perlas stored a sizable supply of booze under the seats of the Jeep.

They made it safely to the area of the village but before they drove up to the restaurant, Sgt. Perlas pulled off onto a secluded beach and parked. The party tipped the bottles of the exotic booze; all the occupants of the Jeep were mellow before starting off again. Then Perlas cranked up the Jeep and headed up a dirt road leading to the village at the far end of the island. After some time, Drago began to wonder if they were lost. There was no light anywhere until they finally spotted a lantern shining in the distance. As they approached it, they saw the light was hung on a tree next to a hut with a thatched roof and clapboard siding. They piled out of the Jeep and were greeted by the proprietor, a toothless bowing Guamanian in Marine khakis...a gift from grateful customers.

A long picnic table filled the room. Another lantern, nailed to a cross-member above the table, lit up the room. Open shutters shed light onto the dense jungle behind the restaurant.

On one side of the table sat four sailors. Three smiling swab jockeys, about the same age as Juarez and Drago, were drunk and they giggled as the Marines entered. The fourth sailor was an immense man seated at the center of the table. He glared at the Marines. His uniform was devoid of any rank. A bad sign, thought Perlas, but he wasn't about to let it get in the way of their mission.

"Howdy, gents," Perlas acknowledged the sitting sailors.

"Gents..." One of the giggling sailors whispered to a buddy. The big man continued to glare as the Marines sat down opposite them.

The toothless proprietor addressed Perlas. "We got T-bones...very best...for officers only." The proprietor would be only too happy to serve up the steaks at two dollars per man. Perlas cocked an eyebrow and mentioned the name of the Seabee Chief Petty Officer who was supplying the joint with fresh meat from Navy stores. Suddenly the price took a nosedive. "OK, OK...fifty cents each. OK?" The Marines smiled. The sailors turned sour.

"Hey you, you old fucking man!" The big sailor in the center seat was incensed. "Why you charging us a dollar fifty and they get it for less? What the fuck is goin' on here?" It was all downhill from there. "That's it!" The big sailor was shouting. "I hate fuckin' Marines! I just got outta the brig, and they beat the shit outta me. Bread and water is all I got the whole time I was in there. I hate fuckin' Marines!"

Perlas wanted the steaks. He was willing to take a little garbage from the garbage sitting opposite, but not much more. Stoyon was ablaze. He gritted his teeth and growled at the grizzly sailor.

"One thing ya gotta remember," he said to the complaining sailor, "is what we learn in the Marines. Don't fuck up, 'cause if ya do, ya gotta pay the price. I ain't been here long or in the Marines long, but I know, like most Marines know, you take your goddamn punishment and shut your fucking mouth!"

The burly sailor rose to the bait. "Oh, yeah? I'll show ya punishment, ya fuckin' dicks!" He was only two inches off the seat when Perlas laid a quick right cross to his jaw. He shook it off. Perlas reared back and clouted the man again, right between the eyes. The sailor blinked, closed his eyes tight and a scorching redness rose from his neck to slowly cover his ears and finally engulf his forehead.

"Oh shit," said Perlas. The Marines rose as one, tipped the table upward and over onto the sailors. They climbed over the table, and the sailors, and out the back window. Perlas was behind the steering wheel already; he threw it into gear. Juarez and Flint barely made it into the back seat as Perlas mashed the accelerator and spun the steering wheel. Stoyon jumped out of the window and landed on the hood of the Jeep. He put his foot on the windshield, and as Perlas took off, he flew into the backseat sprawled across Flint and Juarez. Sirens were beginning to blare as they sped away from the village.

They were long gone by the time the MPs arrived at the restaurant led by a big Marine sergeant who instantly recognized a familiar face among the sailors. He just smiled at the big swabbie and tapped his nightstick on an open palm. It would take a little work to get this guy back in the brig, but the sergeant was looking forward to some fun in making that happen.

The hungry Marines drove back to the secluded beach and settled for a liquid dinner. They still had a considerable supply of green Irish whiskey and other purple and blue intoxicants. The corporals proceeded to get drunk, berating the sailors for keeping them from a tasty meal. Perlas just let it happen. He was thinking that it took some serious balls for young Cpl. Stoyon to confront that huge beast of a man with a hard-on for Marines. Stoyon was quality material, the kind of person needed to be a Sergeant of Marines. The young corporal deserved further consideration.

Signing Up

Drago walked into the battalion office. The first sergeant was thumbing through some papers. The first sergeant was an efficient administrator, well-organized and rugged, a real old salt. The triple A battalion felt like summer camp compared to his previous infantry company. Old now for the corps, and tired, thirty-eight years old with twenty years service, time to retire. He went through the whole war without a scratch. Balding, stout, big framed, still quite muscled, he could still hold his own with the best of them. He never smiled. Drago never saw a first sergeant smile; they were gods in their own environment. Drago placed them in the realm of majesty.

"What's with you, Charlie?" Everyone was Charlie to the first sergeant.

"Patrol," Stoyon said.

"Figures..." The first sergeant pointed at a plump red-headed corporal, known among the battalion as a champion ass-kisser. "Give him your name."

Stoyon approached with distaste. Nobody in the outfit liked the fat corporal, including the first sergeant, but the man could type and file efficiently. The first sergeant didn't abuse his unpopular clerk. He didn't abuse anyone in the outfit, not even Marines he didn't like, but he was perfectly willing to turn over trivial matters to junior men and the patrol roster was clearly trivial in his opinion.

Drago thought he was probably right about the patrol business. *It's a stupid thing to do. Volunteer? Shit, you're a dumb bastard, and getting dumber. Now I gotta ask this turd to put me on the list for the patrol.*

"I'm going on the patrol. What do I have to do?" Drago asked. The clerk shuffled some papers and snickered in a bad imitation of the first sergeant. Stoyon caught the drift and decided the red-headed slob wouldn't make a pimple on the old man's ass.

"You'll have to sign this." The clerk slid a sheet of paper across his desk at Drago.

Stoyon grunted, picked up the paper and studied the heading: "The following men have volunteered for patrol duty." He looked at the names and decided it wasn't such a bad bunch. Cpl. Juarez was there, the man everyone called the Gook. Drago prefered Aztec brown; Gook was derogatory to him. There was P.T. O'Rielly, Jeremy McVey, and Fat Tom, his three his bunk mates. None of them had told him they were going to volunteer. The Guinea from Brooklyn and the two college boys were there. The others were no-names as far as he was concerned

No sergeants, he mused. *They're too smart for this. It's gonna take the rest of us a lot of time to wise up. For Christ's sake, I've to been on this rock eleven months and got seven more to go with nothin' to do, it's gonna drive me nuts. Shit, ya just can't get sit around all of the time. Ya have do somethin'. Six months now and we haven't moved from permanent base camp. Keep movin', it ain't bad. At least you're busy when you're movin' around. Ya could go nuts here. How many times I moved since I been in the Corps? Ten... fifteen? At least Juarez is goin' along. That's good.*

Henry James

Drago, the Croat, made friends easily and lost them quickly. When other Marines got nervous in tense situations, Drago never felt the pressure. In fact, he enjoyed it. Departure from routine never bothered him. Constant movement bothered most people but Drago found himself stimulated by it. Those feeling antsy often looked to Drago Stoyon for comfort. Many times, he just seemed to have the right words to ease their fears. It wasn't something he planned. It was just part of his personality.

The problem was the dependency created would make them shy away from Drago after the situation eased. To have someone to lean on was not in keeping with their supposed impression of themselves. It certainly was not a reflection of the Marine Corps image of self confidence instilled in training. It produced a certain animosity towards the Croat. Just when Stoyon felt a certain kinship with a person it would be lost; they would avoid him.

Henry James was the exception. They became friends aboard the escort carrier that brought then to Guam.

Henry James was from Connecticut. He was long-legged with a neck like Ichabod Crane supporting a small head over a jutting jaw. His complexion was so fair it resembled dried plaster. His blue were eyes set high in his face and close together, making it seem that only the thin bridge of his nose kept them from merging into one big eyeball. His body was gangly and thin down to massive feet that had been a source of much pain and many problems on the drill fields at boot camp.

Henry James was taking his physical after being called up in the draft. The inductees were undergoing a "short-arm" inspection to see if any of them had a venereal disease. A Marine sergeant appeared in front of the draftees and barked, "Anyone here want to be a Marine?" Henry jumped at the invitation. He'd tried to join the Marine Corps before he was drafted but the recruiting sergeant heard him wheezing uncontrollably and sent him home as a hopeless asthmatic. The sergeant standing in front of him at the induction center didn't know that and Henry James was not about to tell him.

What the recruiting sergeant did know was that Henry James didn't look like Marine Corps material. On the other hand, mounting casualties in the Pacific were creating higher demands and somewhat lower standards. Pride and glory through service in the Corps were costly commodities and volunteers were few and far between at this late stage of the war. The sergeant accepted him on the spot and that was fortunate for Henry James. If he'd had to stay and complete the physical exam, he would have been classified 4-F.

Henry and Cpl. Drago Stoyon became pals aboard ship. They spent a lot of time just talking. When Drago said something that Henry James found funny, he'd laugh until he started wheezing and gasping for breath. Henry worked in a gas station. A co-worker chided him about his gangly stature and then mimicked an asthma attack. Henry went along with it and even helped perpetuate the caustic imitation, up to a certain point. If he thought they were making a fool of him he would lash out and gave his tormentor a little taste of a serious breathing problem by choking him half to death. A customer waiting for an attendant to give him a dollar's worth of gas entered the station and saved Henry from a homicide beef. The guy was able to pry Henry's hands away from the other attendant's throat.

Drago Stoyon saw that side of Henry James. When trouble was brewing, Drago would often take a tormentor aside and tell them the gas station story with allusions to a certain degree of insanity that made Henry a dangerous enemy. A fight was usually averted and a legend was quickly built among the Marines aboard ship. Henry James was a dangerous man to cross. Drago was his friend and he brought peace into Henry's life. He felt obligated to Drago.

Marines whispered for fear Henry James would hear. "There's the nut," they'd say pointing at Henry. "That's the only guy that can stay around him." They would indicate Drago Stoyon and shake their heads. "Anyone else comes near him and he goes off his crock."

Drago enjoyed time spent with Henry James who he discovered had a quick and deep intellect. Henry grasped scientific concepts and explained them to Drago in simple, understandable terms. It was like going to school for Drago, except this time he could actually learn something.

"Points of stress," he said. "All things have a point of stress. In extreme conditions, those points often disintegrate."

"Is that right, Henry?" Drago Stoyon just nodded with a big smile on his face.

The Mess Sergeant

Henry and Drago stood at ease side-by-side on the flight deck as the carrier maneuvered into Apra Harbor, marveling as the bridge crew steered the big ship around battle debris. A harbor pilot finally got the carrier nestled up to a pier and they stood looking at the destruction wrought by furious Japanese and American air attacks on the island. Guam had been taken a year before they arrived. Seabees had torn out all the shattered berthing facilities and created new docks to receive the huge influx of supplies that were required to support the war efforts elsewhere in the Pacific. All that was crucial before the war ended.

It seemed like massive overkill now that Guam had become merely a staging area for thousands of Marines waiting to rotate home. They were orphans out here; their divisions and regiments mostly disbanded. Most were headed home; others were being assigned to occupation outfits. Drago Stoyon, Henry James and the new Marines aboard the carrier were just beginning a peacetime tour of duty in the Marianas with no mission beyond stabilizing the situation on Guam.

They disembarked from the carrier and were ushered to a flat piece of land lying to the left of the harbor. All classification according to military occupation or training was abandoned. They were just names and numbers to be slotted into a personnel roster in alphabetical order. Forty men for island supply command; forty more for Military Police duty and so it went down the alphabet from A to Z. Never mind where you were going, just fall in with a designated group when your name was called. Then it was stand by until trucks came to haul them away. *That's the way it is with replacements*, thought Drago. *You're all like black sheep groping, maneuvering for a slot in a new outfit. What the hell? Sometimes ya fit, sometimes ya don't. Whatever, I'll make out all right.* They waited for the trucks with bed rolls, duffle bags, packs and rifles always close at hand. They carried field transport packs with shelter halves covering blankets wrapped in a horseshoe shape around their haversacks. If you pushed them together you might make something resembling a bed.

Just like a relaxing chair in the shop window at home, Drago mused as he stretched out on a pile of gear. *Like one of them green leather things they call a recliner.* He relaxed and plopped his steel helmet on his stomach, feeling the ocean breeze off the harbor. *Not bad here. Cool breeze off the ocean, clean air, not salty or sticky.* He stretched the muscles down the length of his body, closed his eyes and imagined himself in a recliner. Drago had a way of making fantasy work for him even under the most adverse conditions.

It was different for Henry James, who had been separated by the alphabet from his buddy. He spent a lot of sweaty time struggling with all his gear through a milling mob of Marines until he finally found Drago, dropped his gear and plopped himself down on the pile of packs. They had just been issued a quick meal of cold coffee and rock-hard biscuits.

"Piss-poor meal after the chow on that carrier." Drago commented. Peterson and Sylvester, brand new buddies from the arbitrary assignment process, were bitching about the chow and speculating about what the mess sergeant could do with the biscuits he handed out to the new arrivals.

"We coulda stoned that bastard to death with 'em." Peterson was talking to no one in particular but it was clear who he meant. There was a heavy-set sergeant meandering through the sprawled crowd tossing biscuits. His girth indicated he had more to eat than he was willing to share with the new arrivals. "About ten hits from this hardtack and that fucker would be dead and gone."

Sylvester nodded at the fat mess sergeant and tossed a stale biscuit from hand to hand. "Feed him more than two of these fuckin' things and they'd tear up his bowels. That fat yardbird would bleed outta his ass for a week."

"Well, it ain't gonna be no bed of roses now that the war's over." Peterson stood and stretched. "We ain't nothin' but a bunch of turds out here." He picked up a rock and tossed it casually toward the mess tent.

"You shoulda ate that rock," Sylvester commented. "It'd taste better than these fuckin' biscuits. Outfit that shit-canned that stew-burner must have had a party when his orders arrived."

Cpl. Drago Stoyon tried to shut it all out and ignore the useless bitching. *Sometimes they just ought to suck it up and let it be.* He closed his eyes and dozed.

Henry James sat listening. Then he began to giggle and wheeze. Peterson had never seen that act before. He nudged Stoyon out of a doze and pointed at Henry. "Get a load of this guy. Look at him, will ya? He's gonna bust a gut."

Drago had been dreaming that he was digging a foxhole on some contested beachhead where the sand was so soft that he could make no progress with the entrenching tool. The sand he tossed out of the hole kept spilling back in and he became furious, pushing and shoving at the uncooperative sand with his hands and arms. *Don't look up; concentrate on digging. If ya look up a sniper is gonna spot ya.* When he finally felt Peterson's elbow, Drago snapped awake and grabbed for his rifle. "What the hell's goin' on? What'd you do that for?" He glared at Peterson, clutching his rifle and ready to use it.

Peterson was over the fascination with Henry James and his asthmatic laughter. He had a new target demanding attention. He pointed at an officer with the silver oak leaf of a lieutenant colonel on the front of his utility cap. The officer was knee-deep in an ass-chewing session with the fat mess sergeant as his victim.

"Look at that light colonel reaming that fat bastard a new asshole. Bet he pulls them stripes right off his dungarees."

Drago set his rifle aside and wiped at the crust in his eyes. He was annoyed at being disturbed for a moment and then focused on the little drama being played out among the replacement Marines. The mess sergeant was the center of everyone's attention. He had a pot belly stretching a sweat-stained dungaree shirt with six stripes painted on the rolled-up sleeves. A massive metal serving spoon dangled from one of the meaty hands at his sides.

The unidentified lieutenant colonel was circling the sergeant like a stalking wolf. He had his hands clasped behind his back and was spitting abuse at the mess sergeant every time he passed the man's sweaty face. The irate officer was beet-red in the face and didn't look like he was anywhere near winding down as the sergeant cringed under his tirade. Before long all the new Marines were laughing at the sergeant's situation. They had been in the Corps long enough to recognize a professional ass-chewing when they saw one. Drago nodded at Henry

James and indicated the colonel. "Good deal; good to have a man like that around."

They were too far away to hear all of the dialogue but they could tell the confrontation was reaching a crescendo. "Try...you...do...Mister...Quartermaster...get food... officers' mess...get it there...quick...your business...last time...private...how long in the Corps...never again ...sergeant." It wasn't hard to fill in the blanks as the light colonel drew a final breath and started to move away from the confrontation. His purple complexion was slowly turning to a cool grey.

"There is a lot of shit that goes on in the Corps," Drago said. "But it makes ya feel good to see that light colonel take care of business without calling on some junior officer to do his work for him. I'll take him any time. It ain't all bad, even if ya gotta take some garbage, having somebody straighten out the shit birds for ya. Yeah, he can be my commanding officer anytime. Not that ya got any choice; you take what's handed to ya. Same deal for that colonel. You know he's gotta contend with some pretty dumb bastards."

Stoyon looked at the group of Marines gathered around him. It didn't appear that they understood his comments. They were focused on the mess sergeant who was clearly smarting from such an impressive reprimand in full view of junior Marines. An old salt like him had plenty of experience with ass-chewing but he wasn't happy about receiving one in front of all the assembled replacements. The crappy chow he was responsible for serving was no longer the issue. If he was going to save any face at all at this point, he had to reassert his authority. That meant someone else was going to pay for his incompetence.

Stoyon and his companions watched the fat NCO storm back toward the mess tent and disappear inside. In a very few moments, the sides of the tent were bulging and flapping as the mess sergeant took out his anger and frustration on a crew of innocent messmen. "Wonder how he's gonna make 'em pay?" Drago settled back on his impromptu bed.

"What's 'at?" Peterson wanted more information. "Whatcha mean?"

"Nothin' important..." Drago scrunched around making himself as comfortable as possible. *Maybe the light colonel got bawled out by some two-star general. Maybe he ain't such a big hero.*

Their supper was decidedly better in quantity and quality. Hot beef stew replaced the biscuits and coffee but Drago was in a pessimistic mood. "All ya need is a can opener. Whip out the can opener and look what ya get." He tried to imagine a stateside factory churning out canned beef stew but all he got was an image of the fat mess sergeant standing on a ladder and stirring a huge vat of stew with his big spoon. The cook had the same hurt look on his face as he displayed when the light colonel walked away from the impressive ass-chewing.

Cry, he's gonna cry, Stoyon thought. He smiled at the image and began to giggle.

"What's the shit-eatin' grin about?" Henry James was puzzled but also smiling.

"I was thinking of the look on the sergeant's face when the colonel finished reaming him out." Drago erupted into laughter and Henry James laughed right along with him. Before long they were both rocking back and forth, convulsed with giggles. Stoyon spilled some of his stew but it didn't bother him. "It don't matter, Henry. There's more where that came from."

A half-hour later, a gunnery sergeant showed up and told them to board trucks waiting near the road. Drago said goodbye to Henry James; they shook hands. They were not to meet again for some time but when they did, the encounter would add substance to Sgt. Perlas's assessment of Cpl. Drago Stoyon.

Orote Point

Drago Stoyon and his fellow replacements wound up at the 9th Antiaircraft Battalion which was emplaced on a long sloping stretch of land east of Apra Harbor. The position was on the south side of Guam's Orote Peninsula, where a base camp constructed on a flat plateau was encircled by high cliffs. Rocks below the cliffs were pounded by relentless waves, creating a constant roar heard on the cliffs and camp.

The camp was mostly empty when they arrived. They were greeted by a heavyset staff sergeant with raven black hair and a matching mustache. Mustaches were not seen often in the Corps. Facial hair was frowned upon. Those who deviated from the norm were reprimanded, except when prior deeds exempted them from conformity. The staff sergeant, in Drago's mind, had paid his dues.

The NCO had a southern drawl. His dark swarthy skin was in contrast to the fair complexion of the southerners he knew; the sergeant didn't fit. He reminded Drago of some Virginia coal miners he'd seen stateside. A lot of Italian immigrants wound up working in Virginia and West Virginia mines. Stoyon thought the sergeant might be one of those.

"My name is Sergeant Braxton," the NCO announced to the men who had been delivered to him. *More to consider*, thought Stoyon. *Braxton ain't an Italian name.*

Without much more to say, Sgt. Braxton led the new men toward a block of squad tents and assigned them to vacated bunks under canvas. Each man was filling a void left by men returning to the states. Drago dropped his gear and looked around the interior of his assigned tent.

Home, he thought. *There's long way to go before I rotate...just finished six months with the division. That leaves eighteen months right here before I finish my tour.* There were times when Drago envied short-timers. They'd already finished their tour on the rock where he was now stationed. Most of them were reservists signed for the duration of the war plus six months and they were headed home for discharge. Drago was a regular and had to do his time wherever the Corps sent him for the entire duration of his enlistment. He had to endure.

Drago met Peterson as he was on his way to the camp shower. The plumbing was not unusual due to the circumstances. It was just a 55-gallon drum supported on a two-by-four frame. That drum was kept filled by a series of pipes connecting it to a second drum on the ground, filled with water, which was equipped with a pump. First you had to pump water into the top drum. To use it, a man simply stood under the barrel and pulled on a rope that released water through a nozzle. The only resemblance that fixture had to true plumbing was that it sprayed the occupant as long as he held it. You stood there with rope in hand as the whole world watched you suds down in your naked magnificence.

"It's like you're on a stage for the whole world to see," Drago told Peterson.

As they washed, a whistling sound distracted them. They ignored it until it happened again, louder this time. Neither man could identify the sound but Drago thought it was somehow vaguely familiar. He just could not place it.

They had almost finished when a spray of rock shards erupted from the cliff behind the shower and smacked into the wooden beams supporting the water drum. They grabbed towels and retreated toward the tents in a hurry.

As they passed the Quonset hut that served as their area mess hall, a heavyset Marine exited drying his hands on a towel. "Well, who are the dashing Greek gods we have here?" His voice contained a soft southern twang.

Stoyon was meeting one of his bunk mates for the rest of his time on Guam: Fat Tom.

"What have we here, recruits?" He eyed the two new arrivals with towels wrapped around their waists. "What's your hurry? There ain't nowhere to go but right here."

"Hey listen, I may be wrong," Stoyon nodded in the direction of the shower, "but I think somebody was shooting at us while we were in the shower."

"Is that all?" The Marine began to chuckle. "It's that damn old Jap hermit at it again. He's been up in those rocks so long, most of us forgot about him. He ain't much problem anyway. Some say he's got friends among the local gooks and they send him food at night. Nobody knows how he got up in them rocks. Ain't no access road. He's been around since the island was secured. One time they had a destroyer come by and try to blast him out of his hole. He cranked off a round and nicked one of the officers standing on deck. We ain't seen that destroyer since. Usually takes the old fart about three rounds to dial it in. How close did he get this time?"

"He splintered the wood above the shower," Peterson reported.

"He's gettin' better," Tom said. "Last time he unloaded a magazine before he got anywhere near. Most times he misses by a mile and them rounds just whistle right on by."

Tom was wearing a big smile and didn't seem at all concerned about a Jap renegade taking the unit's shower under fire. Drago figured it was a bit of a show.

Fat men always have to be smilin' and laughin', he thought. *They always seem to put up a false front. I'll keep an eye on this guy. He'll drop his guard one of these days. They run deep, these fat guys.*

Dewey and Pete

"Pete," Dewey said, "let's get them dogs out of the pen and do some 'coon huntin'. We'll take the blue tick and the gray...aw, shit...let's bring 'em all along." Pete opened the pen and the dogs scattered, baying in expectation of the hunt. They herded the dogs, leashed them and off they went.

Pete enjoyed hunting with Dewey. It was a rare day they didn't come back with meat when Dewey was on the trail. Pete knew his friend was persistent chasing down a 'coon. There were times he even outran the dogs. He could finish off a raccoon with a knife or bring down a buck with a rifle at a hundred yards. As a hunter, Dewey Braxton had no match in the county.

Hunting was more a necessity than a pastime in the Braxton family. At the tail end of the Great Depression, they were losing their farm near Clarksville, West Virginia. Dewey found out just how bad things really were one day when he encountered his father sitting in a rocker on the front porch. He'd just entered their yard when the old man called him. Since the old man rarely talked to Dewey, it was bound to be something significant.

"Things is bad boy," his father said. "You're sixteen. Best you go off on your own."

Dewey was stunned but his father had more to say. "I'm gonna pack up and travel west with ma and the younger boys,"

Just like that, Dewey thought. *I'll be damned. What about me? I don't have any more family. No place to live. How can they do this to me? I'll never forgive the old bastard. I ain't garbage to be abandoned.* The more he thought about it, the angrier he got.

"Travel well, boy." His father rose and waved as he walked away from his oldest son.

Unsure about what he should—or could—do about his situation, Dewey went to see his best friend. Pete traveled the country on the bum, following the crops, looking for work. Pete rode the rails, and Dewey decided to follow suit.

"I need your help Pete. I need to know about riding the rails."

"Shit, Dewey..." Pete said softly, barely looking up from the rifle he was cleaning. "Ya cain't go off on your own. Ya don't know nothin' about livin' on the road."

"I'm not stayin' here any longer. I gotta find work. You gonna help me or not?" Dewey grabbed the rifle from Pete.

"Damn, ya asshole. I ain't gonna let you wind up in some 'bo jungle all alone. You'd get scraped raw by them bums." Pete made a move to retrieve his rifle; Dewey wouldn't let go.

"Besides, the marrow in my bones is churrnin' to go. Ya got company," said a smiling Pete.

They took off in May, picking strawberries along Route 17 in North Carolina for three cents a quart. Farther south it was peaches in Georgia at five cents a bushel. Pete and Dewey headed north and settled into a hobo jungle in Charleston. They wound up getting robbed by a knife-wielding bum. The thief was a huge beast of a man. Nobody in the hobo jungle was willing to give them a hand for fear of retaliation. Dewey and Pete left the sanctuary. Being robbed was too shameful for them to stay after that incident but Dewey called a halt on the outskirts of town.

"Pete. I'm goin' back there," he said.

"No, you're not!" Pete put a restraining hand on Dewey. Dewey shrugged it off.

"Leave go, Pete. Nobody steals from me."

Pete could see it was no use arguing and turned to follow Dewey heading back toward the hobo jungle. As they passed by a lumber yard, Dewey snatched up a two-by-four and told Pete to wait for him. "I'll be back in a bit. You just hang around right here."

The hobos in the jungle melted away from him as Dewey strode into the camp. They all saw the board in his hand and knew what was coming. Some of them smiled. Others sneered. All of them figured the youngster was about to catch a serious beating, board or no board.

The thief was half asleep with his back turned as Dewey approached. When he figured he had a good angle on the man, Dewey raised the two-by-four and brought it down hard. The first blow was right on the top of the thief's head but the man just shook it off. Dewey kept swinging hard and often in a torrent of hard strikes. The big hobo had no chance to get to his feet or put up any kind of defense. In short order, he was bloody and begging for mercy.

There would be no mercy from Dewey. He kept swinging until the man crumpled unconscious and leaking blood into the muddy ground at Dewey's feet. Their money was in the man's pockets. Dewey grabbed it and left without a word to any of the other hobos.

"Damn," Pete said, as Dewey handed him his money.

Neither Pete nor Dewey heard anything more about the incident, but the jungles were alive with the tale of the boy and his vengeance. Dewey became an icon with traveling men.

They rode the rails for three more years, riding freight and baggage. The thrill of the adventure out weighted the times they were hungry.

When the Civilian Conservation Corps was approved by the government, men who had been unemployed and on bread lines through the years of the depression flocked to enlist in their projects. The bo's were no different. Those tired of the day-to-day existence joined. Dewey and Pete also had had enough of the road and joined. Their living standard improved in the CCC. Food was always in ample supply. Dewey adapted well to the strict discipline demanded in the work camps. Pete became dissatisfied and decided to leave. "I've had enough," Pete told his friend. "I'm goin' home."

Dewey stood in front of Pete with his head bowed. "Ya know I have nothin' to go home to. I wish ya the best Pete."

"You too, Dewey." They turned their backs to each other and walked away. It was easier that way.

The CCC camp was run by the U.S. Army. Every once in a while, a Marine corporal showed up at the site. Dewey was impressed by the difference between the soldier's demeanor and the bearing of the Marine. The corporal possessed a confident air rarely seen in most men. He approached the corporal on his next visit and grilled him about the Marine Corps.

The corporal pulled no punches. He told Dewey that the Marine Corps was no CCC camp and Marine Basic Training made strong men cry. When he heard the challenges a recruit faced as a boot, Dewey was impressed. He thanked the corporal for the information.

Dewey would be a Marine; it was just another adventure he wished to add to his life.

Braxton paid his dues

Drago discovered Sgt. Braxton's war experience was right on the money. He heard the story from a guy who had served with Braxton on Saipan. Braxton was with the 17th Defense Battalion assigned to safeguard the recently-captured airfield. While he roamed the perimeter of the air field, the Japanese staged a major attack that broke through the 2nd Division lines and threatened the airfield.

There was no officer around; Braxton took charge. He gathered his men and made them understand that the situation was dire. He instructed them to gather up their rifles and as much ammunition as they could carry, and to follow him. He positioned them where their enfilade fire would do the most damage to the attackers. He rushed from position to position designating fields of fire. Braxton told his gun crew, "There's nothing more ya gotta know. Shoot to kill the bastards. Just line 'em up and squeeze 'em off. Don't move and don't pull back. We got no place to go, so hold tight." Braxton's demeanor and reassuring words did a lot to calm his Marines.

"Banzai! Banzai!" The Japanese came out of the jungle and reached the perimeter air field where the Marines were posted, screaming and firing. The look of intent in their eyes surfaced through the saki and prayer ingested prior to the attack.

Yeah, I remember, Braxton thought. *We stopped the suckers. Banzi my ass.*

Braxton still shivered when he thought about the Japanese officer rushing toward him swinging a samurai sword. As the man approached with the sword raised overhead for a slashing blow, Braxton caught him in the sights of his carbine. The weapon jammed and Braxton could see the look of delight in the eyes of his attacker. Braxton reversed the useless carbine, grabbed the barrel at the nozzle, and waited for his attacker. The Japanese officer swung the sword. Braxton ducked and heard a whistling sound as it passed over his head. At that moment, using the carbine like a baseball bat, he caught the Japanese officer with a vicious blow that broke the man's neck. Braxton killed two more of them, then said, "Three strikes and you're out," and through his terror, he laughed.

The Japanese kept coming and Braxton kept swinging until his carbine broke. Then he grabbed a rifle from a dead Marine and found himself in a bayonet fight with the next man in the assault. He parried a thrust, then dropped the Japanese soldier with a butt-stroke. The attack began to ebb and Braxton made the rounds of his gun crews.

"It's almost over, guys. These fuckers can't keep it up much longer. We'll send these pricks back to their homeland in a shit sack. Just remember to squeeze 'em off."

It was not over. The Japanese massed and attacked again while the Marines poured fire into the screaming throng. Dead enemy bodies piled high in front of Braxton's position before the Japanese finally realized the attack had failed and headed back into the jungle surrounding the airfield.

Braxton checked the positions and discovered he'd lost only two Marines in the action. It was a remarkably cheap price given the huge number of Japanese dead scattered all over the airfield. When he'd arranged for a corpsman to treat the wounded, he wandered off in search of a place to be alone for a while. The adrenaline rush was wearing off and he needed time to think. Braxton found a little cove near the sea and sat. He put his head in his hands and shuddered as he realized the enormity of the attacking force. When he finally calmed down, he noticed there were a number of holes in his fatigues. He found ten, plus one in his canteen and one on his cartridge belt.

Braxton smiled to himself and said aloud, "You are some lucky fuck. God damn."

His men had other ideas. "Did ya see Braxton?" One of his men pointed at the sergeant sitting in the sand. "Jesus Christ, the man has no fear." There were other admiring comments, but Braxton's Marines made no move to intrude on his solitude. Those who knew him cautioned others against any intrusion into his sphere of existence. He could just as well treat his comrades in the same fashion as an aggressor if cornered at the wrong time and in the wrong mood.

He wound up with the Navy Cross for his actions in defense of the airfield on Saipan. With the decoration came a number of secondary privileges including regulations about mustaches. He stood at attention on the airfield as the citation was read to the entire battalion. Braxton didn't hear much of it except for the part about his actions being "in keeping with the highest traditions of the Naval Service." *Traditions of the Naval Service, my ass*, he thought. *The only place we could run was into the sea. That's the answer and why I made 'em hold.*

Sgt. Braxton was a realist. Like most Marines on Saipan and elsewhere in the Pacific, he had certain priorities. There was nothing heroic about the fighting out there. You got on an island and had nowhere to go but forward.

Bunk Mates

Peterson wandered away toward his tent after the sniper incident at the shower. Drago followed Tom and discovered they were bunkmates. It was Drago, Tom and two other Marines under the same canvas.

"Asshole buddies we are," said Tom

"Yours, not mine," Drago said and got a laugh out of Tom.

"What outfit were you with?"

"Charlie Company, 23rd Marines, 4th Division," Drago related. He was proud of that outfit and didn't mind if Tom knew it. He hefted his seabag onto an empty cot and began to unpack.

"You'll like it here." Tom plopped down on his own sack and stretched out. "Ya might get a little rock happy after awhile. Most of the time the old major running this outfit lets ya be. I've been on the island six months now. After the 3rd Marine Division broke up, they sent me to this lash-up. Not enough points to rotate. Gotta finish out my time here on Guam."

Drago knew all about points. You compiled them for time overseas, one point for each month. There were additional points for combat time, decorations, commendations and wounds. If you piled up enough points, they sent you stateside. It worked fine for wartime reservists. Drago was a regular and the point system didn't apply. Regulars served where they were sent until they completed a designated tour of duty. In the Pacific Theater, that was 24 months.

Stoyon reached a level in his seabag where his dress greens were carefully folded. He knew it would be a long time before he needed that uniform, so he stopped unpacking and flopped down on his cot and stared at the canvas overhead.

"Hey, ya like Raisin Jack?" Tom rolled over and pointed in the direction of the mess hall where he indicated some innovative Marines kept a barrel of fruit fermenting into an alcoholic brew. "We got a whole barrel of the stuff cookin' away. All ya gotta do is skim off the gook and you got yourself a canteen cup full of booze."

He smiled all the while he spoke.

Stoyon had experimented with home brewed liquor during his service with the 4th Marine Division. It had not gone well. He remembered that he couldn't remember anything after he'd downed a bunch of the cane squeezin'. The lethal concoction had been distilled from sugar cane and made him deathly ill. He was so sick he fell out of the Jeep he was riding in. The driver, also drunk, didn't stop to pick him up. He lay in the middle of a road until he finally sobered up. Preferring that Tom didn't know that story, Drago lied, saying he'd try some of the Raisin Jack later, and changed the subject.

"Where are the other two guys that bunk here?"

"P. T. and McVey are out polishing gun barrels. They got our 90-milimeters dug in halfway across the island down by Agana and the Quartermaster depot."

Drago had no idea why the guns were emplaced so far away from where the gun crews lived, but he didn't feel like asking about it. He closed his eyes.

"Well, I gotta get back to the mess hall. We got spam tonight." After giving that pertinent information, Tom left.

~~~~~~~~~~~~~~~

Drago was remembering that first day on Guam when the patrol took a break in the cloying jungle. He pulled his sleeve across his sweaty brow but it didn't help. His dungarees were soaked through and as wet as his skin. He mopped at his face with a hand; sweat flew off in a thick spray. Drago watched the men to his front. Tom was getting a laugh out of a few of the men. He held the Thompson machine gun he carried high and away from the men on patrol, knowing the erratic behavior of the weapon. McVey was standing, rifle butt on the ground, hands wrapped around the muzzle. P.T., bleary-eyed, leaned on a tree, rifle slung. Juarez was the point, leading the squad. The two college boys from Brooklyn followed. The lieutenant was fourth. The no-names were scattered about. The crazy Guinea from Brooklyn and the other Thompson machine gun were just in front of Drago: to be watched. Drago was the rear guard.

Drago met Jeremy McVey for the first time about an hour after Fat Tom left for the mess hall on that first day at Orote Point. He'd fallen asleep and was dreaming. In the dream he was sitting in a dark cavern with his legs drawn up against his chest. There was an indistinct figure somewhere in the gloom that kept moaning through hands that covered his face. *That thing is me. What am I gonna do? Where am I going? I don't want to go.* The apparition paced back and forth in his dream never taking his hands away from his face.

"Let me see you!" Drago screamed at the specter. The dark figure slowly lowered his hands but there was no face to be seen. The apparition had a skull covered in textured cheese cloth.

Oh, Christ, Drago screamed in his dream.

He woke, frightened.

He sat up on his cot and tried to shake the images out of his head. "Holy Christ!" He sat with his head hanging until the trembling subsided. Raising his hands to his eyes, he massaged them with his palms. A slight movement to his right caught his eye. He saw a tall, thin Marine sitting on the cot opposite him. It was Jeremy McVey, an oily cloth in hand, vexing the stock on the rifle he held.

"Well now...that must have been a whistler of a dream," the tall man speculated. "Witches and all, I bet. Musta been a real Sleepy Hollow hair-raiser with pumpkin heads and everything."

The man spoke with a bland Midwestern accent and an easy smile on his face. There was no derision in his comments. He seemed to be offering comfort rather than ridicule. Drago decided he liked the man who introduced himself as Jeremy McVey.

McVey was handsome with a thin face over a long, pointed chin covered in bristles that no amount of shaving would hide. He had dark brown eyes under heavy black brows and thick eyelashes. A crop of oily black hair curled around his head. When McVey stood to shake hands, Drago pegged him at nearly six feet tall.

"Yeah, I thought I wouldn't get out of that one." Drago shook his head again and pinched the bridge of his nose. "Boy, dreams can be weird, can't they?"

"Yes, sir," responded Jeremy. "Some like ta scare ya right outta your skivvies. Always good to know ya can get out of 'em."

Drago stretched and paced around the tent aimlessly. "The ones where you're fallin' are the worst. Ya know? When your stomach stays up in the air and the rest of your body is still fallin'? They're the ones that almost make me wet my pants."

Drago knew why his dreams were so disturbing. It was all about Iwo Jima. He was just a replacement, only on the bloody island for a few final days of fighting. Replacements were thrown into the lines like cannon fodder on Iwo. Drago saw four men right next to him get shot in just a few seconds on the line. It was a single burst from a Jap machine gun that killed everyone but him. He laid his rifle on the ground for a moment and was bending over to retrieve it when the machine gunner opened up on them. That's where he learned about luck on a battlefield. He understood the irony; how lucky he'd been at that moment it stayed with him. He went up on the lines, did his job as a rifleman and never shirked, but in the odd moments when he could sleep, the dreams caught up to him.

Drago and McVey exchanged backgrounds. Drago enjoyed listening to Mc Vey talk about his family and life on their farm in Indiana. He could feel the pleasure, love, and pride McVey felt for them during their exchange. Drago noted his easy smile; McVey seemed like a humane person and Drago considered that a good quality in a new friend.

Outside the tent, Marines were returning to the company area from chores or daily duty assignments. It was nearly chow time and Drago could hear messkits rattling as men straggled toward the mess hall. Drago and McVey stood in line until their turn to enter the Quonset hut. Then, they discovered Fat Tom on the serving line. He slapped two pieces of Spam into their messkits and warned them to chew it thoroughly. Fat Tom said Spam was hard to digest otherwise.

"Anyone who can get this shit down deserves the Medal of Honor pinned on him, on the parade field podium by the general hisself." Spotting the mess sergeant looking his way, he changed his tone and the content of his comments. "Get your fresh cooked ham here. Crisp morsels of the finest pork the Midwest can produce."

When the mess sergeant turned to other matters, Tom made retching sounds and plopped mashed potatoes on top of their Spam. "God help y'all," he said, making the sign of the cross with his big serving spoon.

That caught the mess sergeant's attention and he walked up behind Tom with crisp instructions. "Just put the chow in the messkits, keep 'em movin' and knock off the bullshit."

"Yes, sir. Yes, sir," Tom said with a look of intent on his face as he dished out more potatoes.

Two powerhouses in any outfit, Drago thought: *the mess sergeant and the first sergeant. The first sergeant is*

God's representative on earth and most mess sergeants are the devil by the same token. It was all about power and both of them had the power to make a man's life miserable.

~~~~~~~~~~~~~~

McVey was the kind of guy who needed solitude. He always tried to find himself a quiet place to think in the evenings. He always managed to escape from the noise and activity of the company area and found a spot in a grove of trees that lined the cliffs and sat with his back to a tree enjoying the comfort of being alone. He spent that time thinking about his home in southern Indiana and his family.

Back home at this time of year, he thought, *the wheat is golden, floating in a cool breeze. The grass is green and the leaves are starting to fall from the trees.*

McVey remembered similar times when he'd sneak off after school and sit with his back against a hardwood tree on a hill near his home and just dream, and look the land over the fields a patchwork of winter quilts, comforting. The high clouds of fall singed from orange to deep purple. He enjoyed it all.

At the quiet times, he'd remember laughing at his sister with jam smeared on her face from ear to ear. He'd think about horsing around in the barn. When they were too tired to play anymore, they'd just collapse into a pile of fresh hay. Mealtime: Mother McVey laughing, hugging, teasing; father maintaining a stern expression, feigning a cough into cupped hands to hide his mirth. At times, leaving the kitchen to the back porch, unable to control his laughter.

There was a lot of love in that old farmhouse. McVey remembered his Mom and Dad sitting on the porch, looking out over their property and planning the next day's work. Mom would run her hand through Dad's thick black hair. Dad would kiss her neck. *Lots of love and lots of laughter,* McVey remembered those days before the Marine Corps, before Guam.

During those quiet times, McVey sat listening to the surf roll up and recede on Guam's beaches. He was at peace...for a time.

Fat Tom

Tom was not really fat, but he had a distinctive roll of pudgy flesh around his midsection and that was enough to earn him the nickname. The rest of his body was well-muscled, sitting atop two toothpicks that passed for his legs. His bright blue eyes were accentuated by his red face. Fat Tom's skin didn't tan. When he worked outside under the broiling sun, he just got redder by shades. He had a moon-shaped face; the only flaw in its symmetry was a pin-pointed chin. A permanent smear on his lips resembled an abrasion on a pear. A goiter-type protrusion in his bulging neck in conjunction with the rest of his body made Drago think of a Kewpie doll.

It wasn't Fat Tom's bizarre appearance that bothered Drago. In the Corps there were a lot of odd-looking people but they always fell into two categories: Those that could save your ass and those that would get you killed. Drago wasn't sure which way Tom might go in a pinch. He'd resolved to keep a close eye on Fat Tom. The guy always seemed to be trying to prove something. Drago wasn't sure what that was and he wasn't about to make a decision until he found out.

Early on, Drago figured him for a nut job. Lots of Marines put on that kind of act to impress replacements. It gave them veteran status among their peers. Drago understood that kind of thing, but Fat Tom sometimes did things a veteran would never do. There was a time when they were walking through a major battle site on Guam. It was different than most of the battlefields on the island...most were sandy beaches backed by dense jungle. This area was covered with small saplings. Fat Tom suddenly bent and picked up a small tubular casing off the ground.

"Now, what have we here?" he said, shaking the tube back and forth next to his ear. Drago could distinctly hear something rattling inside the tube. Drago was ready to hit the deck as he recognized what Tom was holding. The tube bore the white bands of a Japanese mortar round.

"God damn you, Tom! Put that thing down! You lookin' to blow your fool head off?"

Drago backed away but Tom just kept grinning and shaking the mortar round. *If that thing goes off,* Drago thought, *it'll be all over for both of us and that dumb bastard will wind up with his brains splattered all over these trees. He's a fucking nut case.*

Drago stood his ground in spite of the danger. That was part of the code. Guys didn't show fear even when they felt it the way he did at that moment. Fat Tom walked toward him still jiggling the mortar round and grinning like a kid with a new toy.

"Boy, whatsa matter? Ya scared? Ya got 18 months to do on this rock and it won't be long before you're wishin' this thing would go off." He started to giggle and then casually tossed the mortar round over his shoulder. It slithered off one of the saplings and Drago flinched, waiting for a detonation. "Boy, you gettin' nervous in the service."

"That damn thing coulda been live," Drago was making a decision about Fat Tom. "You coulda got us both killed, you dumb sonofabitch."

"Well, if that happened..." Fat Tom made a sad grimace that was immediately replaced by his characteristic grin. "Why, then we'd both be headin' for the happy hunting grounds."

Drago decided he was going to avoid Tom on any further excursions. *Man like that could get ya killed. I'm gonna steer clear of this bird. I've got a life to live and a prick like that ain't gonna take it away from me.*

~~~~~~~~~~~~~~~

Hey there, Joshua!" Tom called to the man walking toward him as he sat in the back of his father's truck worrying a plug of chewing tobacco. Joshua approached with a wave and Tom offered him the plug of chew. Joshua whipped a switchblade knife out of his jeans and pared off a portion of tobacco for himself.

What you doin' here in town, Tom?" Joshua slipped the chew into his cheek and replaced his knife. "We don't see y'all that much anymore."

"Daddy and me just come in to pick up some shot. Lots of deer up where we live and season's about to open. We're lookin' to get us some table meat pretty soon." It was as good a reason for a rare visit to town. Tom and his father rarely came in from their place on the outskirts. Mostly town people came to them with scrap metal to sell at their junkyard. Tom and his Daddy owned twelve acres of very valuable trash, what with wartime scrap drives.

"Darned hot to be goin' to the flats this time of year," Joshua said and pointed with his thumb over his shoulder. Tom nodded and worked the chew around his dry mouth. It was muggy and stifling in their part of North Carolina for mid-November. Joshua wandered away with a nod and Tom peeled off the thick wool sweater he'd put on before they left the scrap yard. They had a good business going at the end of 1944 but it wouldn't be long before Tom would have to go in the military. He was thinking about the Marine Corps but Daddy wanted him to say home for as long as possible. "We got us a gold mine," the old man said and he was right. Scrap metal was at a premium during wartime and they were getting lots of it to sell these days. Most days Tom would meet people looking to sell scrap at their yard. He'd weight it up and dole out cash at a penny a pound. Other days he and Daddy would hitch-up the horses to their wagon and make the rounds of the countryside looking for scrap metal. They left the truck home. Gas rationing the way it was, if they had to use up the ration cards, it was better to save it for the trip to the mills. They'd spot scrap on some old farm and low-ball the farmer for it. When the farmers squawked—and most of them did—Daddy would just start talking about how sacrifice was everybody's patriotic duty. Most of the time they relented, and accepted the paltry sum.

Daddy loaded up the truck and took the scrap to the mills in Pennsylvania where they got five cents a pound for it. It was a good, steady income.

Tom hated working in the junkyard. He'd much rather be deer hunting somewhere out in the woods. If it just wasn't for his daddy. He remembered the buck he'd bagged last season. It was a big whitetail that came bustling over a rise right in front of his stand. The wind was in Tom's face so the buck didn't catch his scent. Tom drew down carefully and fired a solid shot. He was elated and stood watching as the animal thrashed and bled on the ground. He'd missed his aiming point. The buck was still very much alive. As the deer struggled, Tom reached for his skinning knife and moved to avoid the thrashing hooves. He grabbed the antlers and put a knee on the animal's neck. Then he pierced the skull and killed his first deer.

He tied the deer's back legs to a tree branch and was about to make an incision to cut out the intestines of the deer. His father sat in the bed of the truck and watched. Tom was being careful not to pierce any of the buck's internal organs with his knife as he ripped down the animal's belly. He jumped back in shock as all the guts splashed onto the ground at his feet.

"Shit!" He screamed dancing away from all the blood and slime.

"I told ya," his father said. "Ya gotta ream his ass hole first; I told ya that."

It was always the same with his father; he railed his son after the fact. Tom constantly searched his mind for the implied instructions, and found none. The censure was his father's way of putting his son's confidence at bay. His father did not wish to stand second to his son. The youngster understood. He looked up from his task, smiled with that curling of his lips he used to let the world know that he had them figured out.

He looked away from his father and reamed the deer. His blade was sharp; he went about skinning the deer with little effort. The blood on his hands summoned thoughts of another blooding this past summer.

Rose Ann

Joshua and Tom sat in his father's truck at Fletcher's Landing, watching the tide roll out. A cool breeze from the muddy marsh kept the summer heat at bay. Coming out of a strand of trees, Rose Ann appeared. She stopped when she saw the truck.

"Hi, Rose Ann!" Tom leaned out a window and waved her over toward the truck. "Whatcha doin' here? You goin' somwheres?"

Rose Ann didn't move so Tom ground the truck into gear and steered it toward where she stood. She wore spiked heels with straps running up her calves to a point just under a pair of peach-colored culottes. The rest of Rose Ann was covered by a sleek white blouse with billowing sleeves that covered her arms down to nails polished a bright pink.

Rose Ann was not a whore, she just liked to be fondled and fucked. Every boy that made overtures to her knew they had to ply her with words of endearment in order to get into her pants. It didn't matter how many were lined up, the prerequisite to plunging required a lot of sweet talk.

"Ya know I love ya, darling." Tom started the ritual as Rose Ann smiled and waited for more. Tom took the cue. "I've been dreamin' about ya. My heart aches for ya. I can't control myself. Folks see me and think I got a sledge hammer in my drawers. Ya just can't understand how embarrassed I am about it. But you're there all the time, my lovely sweet potato."

Rose Ann smiled and hopped on the truck's running-board. She opened the door and pulled Joshua out of his seat so she could sit between the two boys. Tom and Joshua each grabbed a thigh and a breast. Tom clucked, crowed like a rooster and kissed Rose Ann on the neck.

"Oh, Tom!" Rose Ann said, and then she grabbed both of them by the crotch. Tom crowed louder bringing a delighted grin to Rose Ann's face. Then she sighed and as quickly as she'd enjoined their parts she released them both.

"Damn, Rose Ann! Ya know I love ya!" Tom pleaded, assuming Rose Ann needed a little more persuasion. Joshua was sitting mute. Tom gave it another try. He ran a hand up her thigh and began to massage her silky mid-section. It didn't help.

"No, Tom," Rose Ann was adamant. "I can't, you know...I got my *thing*."

"Damn, Rose Ann, I don't know what you're talking about." Before Rose Ann could say anything further, his hand wandered, broaching the waistband of the culottes, and slid easily down until he felt her pubic hair. His paw plunged deeper down into her crotch. Rose Ann gave into his probing digits. As Tom came close to the prize his fingers became immersed in a liquid he did not remember coming into contact with before. There's something wrong here. He stopped his probe, flexed his fingers, wondering what he'd encountered.

"Now... ya see?" Rose Ann said, as the ecstasy that gripped her was negated by the odd expression on Tom's face.

"I told ya I got my *thing*!"

"Fer Christ sakes, Rose Ann! What the hell you talking about?"

Tom pulled his hand from her pants and gawked at the blood on his fingers. "Holy Mother of Jesus, Rose Ann! You're bleedin'! What happened? We gotta get you to a hospital! Look at the blood! You're gonna die!" Before Rose Ann had time to explain, Tom turned the truck engine on and sped off in the direction of Elizabeth Town Hospital. "Don't you worry, Rose Ann, we're gonna get ya some help right away."

"God damn, Tom, are you crazy?" Rose Ann recovered her composure and started screaming at him. "I don't need to go to the hospital! Are you just out of the looney bin?"

"Never you mind," Tom said, mashing the accelerator to the floor. "We're rushing as fast as we can. We'll get ya to the hospital quick."

"Joshua," Rose Ann screamed, "tell this son of a bitch what's happening!"

Joshua smiled; his eyes were so filled with mirth he thought he would burst. Rose Ann became more furious as Joshua's grin spread. She'd get no help from him. "All right, ya idjit... but wait till you get to the hospital. You'll wish you hadn't been such a damned fool."

Tom steered the truck up to the hospital's emergency entrance, grabbed Rose Ann and dragged her through the doors. He found an orderly and began shouting. "Help! She's bleedin' to death! Get her some help!"

The orderly called the intern on duty while Rose Ann just sat on a gurney, her decision not to say anything more burned into her mind. An intern rushed into the emergency room, looking for someone near death. He didn't see anything remotely resembling that situation. "What's the matter here?" he asked.

"She's hurtin' real bad," Tom told the doctor pointing at the girl on the gurney. The intern clearly didn't see any evidence of that. He approached Rose Ann and asked her what the trouble was.

"That's the trouble," Rose Ann said, pointing to Tom. Rose Ann grabbed the intern's jacket and pulled him closer to her where she could whisper in his ear. The intern listened and then frowned. So...what's the problem?"

"Ask that stupid fool over there." Rose Ann jerked a thumb in Tom's direction.

The intern turned his attention to Tom. "Well?" he said, leaving Rose Ann and approaching Tom.

"She's gonna bleed to death, ain't she? I've done hurt her. I'm awfully sorry. Don't let her bleed no more. Please, Doc."

The doctor just shook his head and faced Rose Ann. "Didn't you tell him what was going on?"

"Well, Mister..." Rose Ann glared at the doctor and hopped off the gurney. "You just should have been there to hear that damn fool wail about me dying."

The intern turned to look for an explanation from Tom just about the time Joshua collapsed against a wall roaring with laughter. He howled until he was gasping and then slowly slid down the wall until he was flat on the emergency room floor.

Tom stood there, mouth agape, at a loss to understand the reason for the laughter when someone was bleeding to death.

The intern turned around from the three who caused this classic farce, and raised his arms in disgust. Then he looked at each of the players, while the girl stood by the gurney, hands on her hips, glaring at them all. Joshua, holding his side, was laughing so hard it pained him. He started to tear. Tom looked to all of them as if to say, "What's wrong here." His face had the look of someone reeling in a fish, just to have it disengage the hook when within grasp.

The intern left them mumbling to himself.

It wasn't long before the whole town heard the tale of Tom and his encounter with Rose Ann and the blood. On his occasional trip to town, he'd see those congregated with smiles on their faces as he passed them in the truck. Bloody Tom it was and would be from then on. About that time the sneer, the curling of the lip became part of his constant expression.

There was an incident on Main Street. Tom and Joshua were talking with a bunch of friends when one of them asked to see Tom's hands. Tom complied wondering what the guy was looking for as he held his hands out for inspection. "Just wanted to see if you got any pussy lately," the boy said and immediately wished he hadn't. Tom beat him to the ground and then stomped him for good measure. Joshua finally caught him in a bear hug or he might have killed that kid.

~~~~~~~~~~~~~~

As he cleaned the deer, Tom wiped his hands on the sweater he wore. Crimson streaks held fast, as did the memory of Rose Ann. Blood would again soil his hands and enter his soul in the Marine Corps and stay with him for the rest of his life . He would sigh as the memory of it came to him.

Tom despised the junk yard. "I'm a prisoner here and the old man is my keeper." The penny pinching and slovenliness degraded him. At a time when he could be exempt from military service by being employed in a wartime industry, he made his decision to leave.

"You're gonna be sorry," his father bellowed. "This is all gonna belong to you some day." That made absolutely no difference to Tom. It was likely an empty promise anyway, so he decided to follow the path his mother took shortly after he was born. He'd just leave without fanfare. At this point, he had a lot more understanding of why she might have done that. She'd likely had all the emotional abuse she could stand and so had Tom. "Take this miserable existence and go to hell with it!" Tom told his Daddy. "You can take all of it and the money that goes with it and dump it in the fuckin' shithouse! This ain't no place for a man. So long, old man!"

Tom packed a bag and boarded a train out of Elizabeth Town bound for Parris Island, South Carolina. He hadn't enlisted but that didn't matter. He was determined to become a Marine. When he got to the gate at the base, that's what he was going to tell them.

Drago's Dilemma

Tom, McVey and Drago went to the movies, but finding three empty sandbag seats was a real chore. Nearly every good seat was occupied and they had to wander the area to find three seats next to each other. About that time it began to rain. As usual for a night at the movies on Guam, they'd brought their ponchos and helmets so the rain was no real problem. Once you were there, you didn't leave no matter how bad the film or the weather.

The movies always brought home a little closer. There seemed to be something in every film that you could associate with home. If the movie was a real loser, most of the audience just stared at the screen and dreamed. It was an effective way to combat tedium on the post-war Pacific island.

Not that Guam was bad as Marine Corps assignments overseas went in 1946. In fact, compared to other islands being occupied by Americans, Guam was as close to an Island paradise as you could get. The temperature hovered around 80 degrees nearly every day all year. There were cool ocean breezes and very little humidity around the island perimeter. Everyone was tanned and healthy-looking after a short time on the island. Almost everything standing was made in the States including most of the native quarters. If you ignored the dense jungle of the interior, you could easily imagine you were stationed in southern California.

Still, it wasn't home. Although you could roam the roads on Guam, all villages were off-limits to service personnel on the island. The only access to them occurred when the USO sponsored a dance. The prettiest women on the island were there, well chaperoned. Truck-loads of military police roamed the area. Twenty women to a thousand Marines did not give anyone favorable odds.

The thought angered Drago as they waited for the show to start.

It was a good movie that evening: a musical featuring Xavier Cugat and plenty of beautiful women. Drago was immediately taken by a raven-haired beauty in a sleek white silk blouse, leaning on a piano, sensually singing a Mexican Ballad. Her bronze skin contrasted with the white blouse she wore, creating an aura of femininity. The white of her eyes encased pitch black pupils, dark enough to brighten paler corneas. She sang softly of Mexican love. Drago didn't mind the rain; it made him feel alive and free. The cool rain running down his neck sent a chill through his body taming the rising emotion he felt for the girl on the screen.

Drago's dilemma regarding women was falling in love with them...all of them. It usually didn't matter whether they were hookers or all-American hometown girls. He fell in love every time. From the prostitute he met in Harrisburg to the gorgeous Jewish girl in Steeltown, women were Drago's weakness. There was something about their femininity, and the sensuality they exuded that captivated him. He couldn't understand it, but there was no question it put a spell on him.

Margie

As the film unspooled and the rain continued, Drago thought about the time he and his buddy Mike Radockovitch joined a bunch of other Serbs out drinking, looking for either trouble or a quick piece of ass. Drago and Mike left when most of them were on the brink of being stupefied; they wandered off alone, and sat down on a curb wondering what to do next. Drago spotted a woman strolling in their direction wearing a fur coat. Flat, sheered, pieced-together skins made it obvious the fur she wore was tawdry. It had a mink collar turned up against her neck and cheeks to ward off the cold. They couldn't see her face. Mike, the consummate whore master, recognized her. He knew her by the way she walked; he was rarely wrong. She continued to approach.

"Hi there, Margie! Where ya been? I've been waiting for ya."

"Say there, Mikey. How are ya darling? You're such a liar!" Mike elbowed Drago and smiled. "We're gonna get laid."

Margie curled a finger at them and they followed to her third-floor flat in a fairly decent neighborhood. They followed her up a few flights of carpeted stairs following a polished mahogany banister to her room. Margie led them inside but kept her coat wrapped tightly around her and made no move to lower the collar that mostly covered her face. Drago still had no idea what she looked like. Mike told him to wait in the bathroom. Drago went in and sat on the commode. Margie finally shrugged out of her coat with her back turned to her visitors.

Gonna get sloppy seconds, Drago thought, *and I don't even know what she looks like. What the hell. I guess Mike he wouldn't steer me wrong.* He sat on the commode for quite a while becoming increasingly nervous and embarrassed. Mike finally jerked open the door with a big smile on his face. "You're up, kid."

Drago entered as Mike closed the bathroom door. He felt so ill at ease he could not look at her and surveyed the carpet at his feet. Finally, he gained enough courage to bring his eyes off the floor. The first thing he noticed was a pair of blazing red patent-leather shoes she had on. As he raised his eyes, he could not believe what he saw. Her body was so well-proportioned it put to shame the Varga illustrations in Esquire. She stood there waiting for him, her body an alabaster so fine it could have been chiseled out of opaque marble. Her breasts were full, veins floated beneath the swells as reeds in a milky cool stream. There were no flaws that he could see in her body; just looking at her excited him, his embarrassment fled.

Finally, he looked at her face. He was so stunned he had to divert his eyes. Her hair covered a portion of her face and when she brushed it back, Drago suddenly wished he was somewhere else. It wasn't that Margie was ugly, but she was definitely odd-looking. Looking at her made him think of a potato left in the icebox too long. Small, beady eyes took notice of Drago's surprise, a fine line of red on her lips curled quizzically; she tilted her head to one side, her expression dog-like, questioning.

Drago couldn't move due to his surprise on seeing Margie's face so Margie took the initiative. She placed one of his hands on her ample breast. The lust that engulfed him after the first contact surprised him. She drew him to the bed; there, he thrust into her. She embraced him as a lover would. He was her lover. He felt passion erupt from her.

"Good God!" He moaned trying to control himself.

"Nice and easy now," Margie whispered in his ear. "Let's make it last. There's plenty of time."

"Jesus, Margie, Jesus!"

"It's okay; it's good, isn't it."

"Yeah, my God!"

"Don't bring Him in on it. It's just plain Margie."

He exhausted himself and slumped down beside her.

"Maybe I'll see you and Mike again some time," she whispered into his ear.

"I don't want to see you with Mike again." Drago propped himself up on his elbows and stared at her strange face, looking into those beady eyes. "I want to see you alone."

"Now sweetie, you know that ain't gonna work, but it's real nice of you." Margie was a working girl and she was in no mood for the sort of commitment Drago obviously had in mind. When he was dressed, she shoved him toward the door, letting her breast brush against his arm and gave him a peck on the cheek. "That's just to let ya know I really like you, sweetie. Goodbye."

Drago and Mike both forked over five dollars and left. Mike was planning the next adventure of the night but Drago couldn't get Margie out of his mind.

Margie was alone. She sat on the sofa, lit a cigarette, and thought about the boy and how he affected her. *Sometimes that happens...it's rare but my god it's marvelous. What is it? I'll never understand it.* She sighed and then smiled.

For weeks he waited at the same spot where he'd first encountered Margie, making sure he was there at the same time every evening, but she never showed. He wound up standing on the street corner and fuming like a lover scorned. He never saw Margie again, but the memory of her body and the way she used it wouldn't leave his mind. It was a glorious encounter but Drago had nothing but memories and frustration to show for it.

Beverly

Another beautiful Spanish singer sashayed onto the movie screen and Drago thought about another time in Steeltown when he'd been taking a short-cut home from the mill by following a creek bed. He was resting on an overpass, his chin propped on his forearms that were folded on top of the guardrail. Staring at the water flowing below him, Drago noticed a young girl heading in his direction. He recognized her as a girl he'd met when he was fourteen and she was twelve.

She had grown into an attractive young woman. She noticed Drago standing by the creek and seemed to be making up her mind whether to continue on her route or stop and say hello. She finally walked toward him. Half way there she stopped, pirouetted, and turned to go back where she started from. Finally, she made up her mind, turned around, and came towards him. He saw eyes that once childishly danced when she was young were now blazingly feminine. Her coal-black hair floated about her shoulders as she walked. She wore a dress cinched at the waist that accentuated the fullness of her breasts and the fine mold of her hips.

He tried to figure out what was so special about her; he could not understand why she, rather than other women, excited him so. He watched her pace as she walked towards him, the way she turned her head, the subtly way she brushed her hair back. Standing still, or placing one foot in front of the other; all her movements made him want her.

"Hey, there..." The girl stopped next to him on the overpass and smiled. "What do you think you are going to find in that stream?"

Drago straightened and watched her full lips moving. He didn't hear a word she said. He mumbled something but there was no way it was coherent. She knew and was pleased that he was enthralled by this chance meeting. When he recovered a bit, Drago managed a smile and nodded toward the water rushing below their perch.

"I'm looking to see your reflection in the stream...just to see if it's as beautiful as you are in person."

She moved closer to the guardrail and peered downward. "Well, what do you think?"

The stream was low; the stones there set up constant V's in the water multiplying as they flowed down to a bend and faded. The reflection was distorted and yet gave him a glimpse of various parts of her that still had a unique beauty even in the abstract.

"It don't make any difference which way I see you," he said. "No matter what form it takes, I still think you're beautiful."

"Thank you." She looked away like she might be thinking of leaving and Drago didn't want that. He was embarrassed about the way he kept staring at her. He wondered if her heart was beating as fast as his. He had to say something to prolong the encounter.

"This is the second time I've seen you. Do you remember about three years ago, you were coming out of your father's store down on Lehman Street? You were so angry about something you didn't see me and damn near knocked me over."

"Of course I remember that day. You hang out with the Serbs on Weidman Street now, don't you? Tony knows you...Tony Dutchaver. He sometimes goes around with the Dabich boys."

"Hey, what are you doing this Saturday?" Drago was desperate to see her again, alone and more intimately. "How about going to a movie with me?"

"That's sweet. Thank you very much...but I'm going out with Tony Dutchaver."

If there was a way he could kick himself in the ass, Drago would have done it right there. He was buried with a knife stuck in his heart. He mumbled something; she felt his distress.

"Please don't be angry," she said. "I'm really flattered that you noticed me."

"Beverly, isn't it? That's your name, right?"

"Yes, and you're Drago. My father knows your father and mother."

"Yeah, they are always in your store. Your people take good care of them."

It wasn't going well and Drago wanted to get it over with before he suffered any further. He stepped away from the guardrail and tried to smile. "I gotta go, Beverly. I have to get home. I'll see ya." Drago dragged himself away from her fighting to retain some semblance of pride after sounding like a love-sick kid. *Christ, what is it she does to me? And I was just standing there looking at her. I think I'm gonna go out of my mind. I've gotta find a way to see her again.*

Drago and Mike went to the Serbian Hall on Sunday with Drago still mooning over Beverly. Mike thought it was bullshit. He didn't love women. He lusted after them. There was no way he could understand what was bothering Drago so badly about a girl he'd barely met. They were sucking on a couple of beers when Tony Dutchaver,

Beverly's steady, came in with Vasa Dabich. They sidled up next to Drago and Mike and ordered boilermakers.

Mike couldn't let the opportunity pass to needle Drago. "Hey, Vasa, guess who's got the hots for Beverly Feinstein?"

"Yeah, I know." Vasa punched Tony Dutchaver on the shoulder.

"Nope...not Tony. It's Drago here." Drago popped a hooker of rye and almost choked when Mike slapped him on his back. "He ran into her last week on Lehman Street and he's been moaning over her ever since. Never even touched her. I could see it if he got into her pants, but she turned him down for Tony."

Tony Dutchaver just laughed. Drago said nothing further about it until he was able to corner Tony alone later in the evening. "No shit, Tony...how do you feel about Beverly? I gotta know. I ain't gonna step on your toes but she's about as beautiful a woman as I've ever seen."

"Hey Drago, I kinda like her," Tony shrugged and pulled at his beer. "But she's a Jew. Nothin's gonna happen between us. She's a Jew. I'm German. You gotta know what that means. Try your luck, if you like."

"I don't get it. She told me she was going with you. I feel like a shithead, but I really like her."

"She said that about me, did she?" Tony assessed the situation with a sly smile. "Kinda changes things. Maybe I got a chance to get into her pants. She's good lookin', but she's still a kike. I'll see how far it goes."

Drago left the hall sober. He wanted to grab Tony Dutchaver and pound some sense into him. He kicked at a garbage can, cursing his plight and Tony's attitude. *Fuckin' Dutchman's playing with her. He don't give a shit about her 'cause she's a Jew, the dumb prick! If I had a chance with her, it wouldn't mean nothin' to me what she is.*

He knew about the anti-Semitism that pervaded the German community. Most of the Serbs were so aligned with the Germans, they followed suit and slandered the Jews; it made him wonder whether being a Croat and a Hunky, he could be maligned also.

Drago began to stalk Beverly. He was totally preoccupied, pining, distracted and losing weight in the process. He parked in front of her father's store, hiding behind a tree. He waited on the overpass by the stream. He never ran into her again. He went into the Marine Corps and other things became more important to him, especially learning to stay alive.

Drago's dilemma with women didn't end when he finally wound up on Guam. The Marine Corps provided distraction that kept him from focusing on passion and there was generally very little contact with women. That didn't keep him from trying. He fell in love with a part Caucasian and Chamorro girl at a dance in Agana.

He spotted the enchanting native beauty from across the dance floor, where he watched her dance with an easy grace. He wasn't the only one who noticed her that night. She was the target of about 200 Marines. The print dress she wore billowed as she twirled around the dance floor. The corporal who had initially managed to get her to the dance was being constantly frustrated by other Marines cutting in for their chance to hold her close for just a moment before the next guy tapped them on the shoulder.

Drago figured her for a Eurasian rather than a pure-bred Chamorro. Pale olive shin encased the body of a sensual beauty. Flowing auburn hair caressed an angelic face; total femininity exuded from that extraordinary creature. Freckles crossing the bridge of her nose sprayed over both her cheeks adding a childish feature to the angel dancing there.

When her partner steered the girl near him, Drago cut in. He was too taken to say much at first. He just stared into her eyes and when she melted against his body, he found his voice.

"Tell me who you are. I've only got about two minutes to get to know you." He pulled her closer and she didn't resist.

"My name is Valeriana Valentine. My mother is Chamorro. My dad is in the Navy aboard a ship somewhere. I don't know when I'll see him again." She seemed drawn to Drago, not at all averse to giving him personal information. Drago was delighted with that although he couldn't figure out why she'd be willing to favor him over all the other guys on the island. Still, there was no denying the close warmth of her body and the way she stroked his hair as they danced around the floor. He didn't want his turn with her to end but he knew it was inevitable.

"Valeriana, we don't have much time here. How can I get in touch with you again? It's really important to me." Before she could respond, the corporal who started the dance with her first cut back in on the moment.

"You can't cut back in...not on the same song." Drago glared at the interloper. "Buzz off!" Valeriana was caught in the middle with Drago holding one hand and the intrusive corporal tugging on the other. She gave Drago a pleading look that silently begged him not to start any trouble. *I'm screwed*, he realized. *I'll never get to know where she lives or how to get in touch with her.* Drago reluctantly let her go and she twirled away in the arms of his replacement.

He thought of Valeriana often during the long hot days on Guam, hoping he might run into her again, but he never did. He caught sight of her just once after that dance and he was too far away to talk to her. She caught his look, waved, and drove on in the passenger seat of a passing Jeep.

The few women he fell in love with exuded femininity...an instant aura that put them apart from other women he came in contact with. He drank them in as an alcoholic drank a shot of booze, or an addict smoked a pipe full of opium. His faith in monogamy was shaken as he realized he could love more than one woman. As their femininity drew him, his masculinity enslaved them. They were trapped by his recognition of their flowering womanhood.

He watched the beauty on the screen and sighed.

After the movie, McVey and Drago trudged toward their tent with rain still bucketing down on them. Walking became a real chore as mud and water squished into their field shoes. They made it to their tent, soaked through. Wet ponchos and helmets were discarded on the deck. Sodden shoes and socks were about to be taken off when Drago heard a gurgling sound coming from the other side of the tent's canvas wall.

"You hear that?" He turned to McVey, waving for him to cross the tent. "Come over here and listen. What is that?"

McVey moved to Drago's side bent down to listen and heard the sound through the tent wall. "I hear it," he said. Disturbed by the sound he rushed toward his footlocker and pulled out his K-Bar, a knife issued to all Marines. Drago grabbed for the bayonet on his cartridge belt hanging from the center-pole of their tent. They ran back out into the rain and headed in different directions to circle the tent and find the source of the weird noise. As Drago turned the back corner, he heard the sound again and paused, kneeling in the mud and ready to spring. *This is some crazy shit*, he thought shaking the mud from his bayonet. *We don't even know what we're facing here.* His heart was pounding. Committed as they were, he hoped his training would take over if they encountered something serious around the next corner. *Gotta be quick*, he told himself, *low thrust and cut upwards right into the bowel. Keep the other hand overhead to fend off counterattack.* He was tensed to spring when he heard a familiar voice.

"I swear, P.T...you scared us half to death!" Drago stepped around the corner and saw McVey shouting at something in the drainage ditch that ran around the perimeter of their tent. When he approached, Drago saw a body prostrate in the mud, face down, arms outstretched with a canteen cup clutched in his left hand and his other hand scrabbling for purchase on a nearby guy-line. The man's face was half-submerged and he made the gurgling sound every time he took a breath. McVey stooped to get a grip on the man, and Drago bent to give him a hand. Whoever the guy in the ditch was, he was no threat. When they managed to turn him over onto his back, the man's mouth opened and muddy water cascaded down his chin.

"Drago Stoyon, I'd like you to meet Peter Thomas O'Rielly." McVey pointed at the prone figure. "We call him P.T., the pride of Chicago's east side."

P.T. smiled a full wide grin, big white teeth glistening as rain cleansed mud from his face. His dark, Romanesque features were splattered with rain. High hallowed cheek bones were covered with thick black bristles from sideburn to sideburn; blue eyes gleamed, engendering fantasy. His near-drowning encased his face in a gray pall that could not banish his winning Irish smile. The hand that held the cup was raised in a toast.

"Gentlemen, here's to Raisin Jack..." O'Rielly slugged from his canteen cup and finished the thought. "May the barrel bubble forever?"

Then he dropped his hand, rolled over and passed out cold. Following McVey's lead, Drago helped get O'Rielly out of the ditch. The man continued to snore through the whole ordeal as they slipped and sloshed through the cloying mud, dragging his dead weight toward the tent. It was difficult; both were encumbered by the blades they carried. They managed to get him inside and dragged him toward the center of the tent where O'Rielly slumped into a disorderly pile of snoring flesh with water pooling beneath his body. Drago and McVey collapsed on their own bunks to rest for a moment and then began to strip O'Rielly down to his skivvies. Picking him up, they dumped the drunk into his cot. O'Rielly didn't seem to notice any of it. He was apparently comatose except for the grin that spread across his face.

"That doggone P.T...." McVey pointed at the figure sprawled on the cot. "He's gonna kill hisself some day. He's been on mess duty at the field camp, when he came back he must have filled his cup in the barrel back of the mess hall. Tom, he put that stuff together. P.T. probably dipped in deep to get the real potent stuff. If we hadn't heard him out there, he might have drowned. Goddamn that Raisin Jack! Daddy made some whiskey back home but it was nothin' like Raisin Jack. That stuff will kill a man!"

Drago just stared down at O'Rielly wondering if the guy would be alive in the morning. McVey reassured him. "He's safe for the night. It ain't the first time for ole P.T. He'll be all right tomorrow."

Drago Stoyon had to admire the snoring drunk in a weird way. *The boy almost killed himself and still he comes up smilin'.* "Hey, Jeremy, take a look at that grin, willya? Looks like he just got laid or somethin'. Did you see him give us a Raisin Jack toast? This guy's a pisser."

~~~~~~~~~~~~~~~~~

"Peter Thomas, you have the wee people in your eyes," O'Rielly's mother said and kissed him on the forehead while tucking the blanket around him. The rotund Mrs. O'Rielly smiled at her third son. *I was small then,* P.T.

thought as he lay on his cot. Peter dreamt; colors darted in and out of his brain from black to purple, shades of white crested to be overwhelmed by the blacks and purples, a kaleidoscope splashing. P.T. put his hands on his stomach. *Sick...oh, lord, I'm gonna get sick. Last time I slept in my own mess. Not this time...gotta get up. No...not yet, not yet.*

In bed in Chicago, Peter rolled onto his side to see his mother at the kitchen table, her work-worn hands cupping her face. Tears streamed through her fingers. It was a sad time for the O'Rielly family but little Peter wasn't sure why the sadness had descended on his mother and his older brothers.

The older boys stood by the coal oil stove warming their hands, whispering words he couldn't quite hear. He could see Patrick talking to Shawn. Sister was asleep in the corner of the room. Peter strained to hear Shawn and Patrick talking. Patrick, his oldest brother, was describing some event he'd seen.

"Fell backwards...arms spread and he seemed to be floatin'. Christ...twenty-one stories! Didn't look scared... he was just floatin'. Don't know how he got on the outside of the safety bar." Patrick shook his head and left his brother at the stove to comfort their mother. Peter Thomas realized they must be talking about father who hadn't come home from work with the older boys. He rolled over and thought about watching them work at sandblasting buildings. They worked up high on scaffolding, wearing masks like doctors as they attacked stone walls with high-pressure hoses. The spray glinted in the sunlight and formed halos around them. Little Peter thought, *They look like angels on high, close to God; they must be close to God and close to heaven.*

There was room on the scaffolding now, room for P.T. since his father was gone. At sixteen, Peter worked as a sandblaster. The work was hard. The mask did not keep out all the sand and grit. It gagged him, burned his insides. The fear of the scaffolding was subdued by the nectar. Chug-a-lugging on Saturday nights. Plenty of money. Tip the shot glass back, burn out the burning in the lungs. Could slip and fall. Old man O'Reilly did; floated down without fear. Their father drank like a fish.

P.T. learned early to subdue fear, but he could not hold his booze like his father, Patrick or Shawn. That was all right. P.T. was allowed the fun of it. Patrick and Shawn drew the responsibility of taking care of the family.

~~~~~~~~~~~~~~

Drago looked the patrol over as they readjusted their gear and got ready to move out behind the point element. P.T. O'Rielly was in the center of the formation. The big Irishman was not so far ahead that Drago couldn't keep an eye on him. P.T. needed watching. Drago smiled as he imagined leprechauns coming out of O'Rielly's ears.

O'Rielly glanced back toward the rear of the formation and caught Drago staring at him. "What the hell are you grinnin' at, Stoyon? You fuckin' Russians are all nuts."

Drago motioned for O'Rielly to move out and stood to follow. "It's that stupid Irish face of yours, P.T. Makes me laugh. Stay alert, shithead. The fuckin' Irish will be the first to go when the revolution comes."

P.T. O'Rielly just laughed, cradled his rifle and walked into the jungle.

Juarez

On this patrol, Drago had a lot more confidence in Juarez. He could see the Mexican up ahead walking cautiously with his rifle ready and his hands in just the right position. Juarez held the weapon easily with his right hand at the stock, index finger poised to flick the safety forward and fall back on the trigger. He cautiously brushed away jungle foliage with his left hand. Juarez was a good man in the bush.

Juarez kept his coal-black eyes roving, sweeping over the areas where jungle growth was thickest, staring into the places where tall trees joined the jungle floor. He was sensitive to it all, looking for differences between movement caused by breeze and rustling in the tall kunai grass that might signal a man crawling into ambush position. He noted the jungle birds thrashing overhead and the animals scurrying out of the patrol's path. Juarez had keen senses and good instincts. He loved this kind of thing for the adrenaline rush it provided. *Listen, pause, look, don't miss a thing*, he reminded himself as he proceeded cautiously. *I'm a Marine. It's my job as a rifleman. This is where I belong.*

What bothered Juarez was his size. He was a big man for a Mexican and this kind of patrol needed a guy who could slither easily through the bush. *I'm too big to be really good at this,* Juarez thought. *Stoyon should be up here. He's not such a big damn target and the little Croat is good. On the other hand, it's good to have him back there as a rear guard. That guy Stoyon is quick, smart: a good Marine.*

Juarez wiped at the sweat streaming off his body and wished he could shed some of the fat he'd picked up after weeks of no patrols and sedentary work around the battalion. *I just turn to blubber,* he thought. *It's always been like that. Carry myself upright and don't slouch, it ain't so noticeable. There's plenty of muscle under the fat but I need to shed some pounds. I'll damn sure sweat some of it off on these patrols...I've got stamina. I can walk all day.*

He took a look at the perspiration streaming off his arms and noted how dark his skin had gotten under the south Pacific sun. The familiar brown tone was damn near black these days. Gook, Juarez thought as he looked around at the white Marines walking behind him. *I'm the gook, the sweet nigger mulatto bastard. Kids used to call me that all the time but not for long. Guy my size don't have to take too much shit. If I take a round up here on point, it won't matter what color my skin is. Blood looks the same drippin' out of a brown guy or a white guy.*

~~~~~~~~~~~~~~

"Juarez...it's Juarez, I'm Mexican."

Pedro Juarez tried to explain it to the three black kids who had him cornered in an alley. He never should have taken this short-cut home but he wanted to get home in a hurry after he finished work at the fish market. Now he was being threatened by three black kids from an unfamiliar neighborhood. They were looking for trouble.

"You a nigger just like us. You gonna tell us you a nigger or else." One of the boys was pounding a fist into his palm. The one in the middle seemed a little more interested in talking than fighting. Pedro focused on him.

"You're just a half-assed nigger. You old lady get mixed up with a white man, that's what she did." Sure as shit, chocolate drop.

The spokesman flaunted Pedro's lighter skin to the amusement of the other Negros.

He had to make some sort of response to their taunts. "What you guys want to bother me for? I didn't do nothin'. Just let me go on home." He made an attempt to pass the menacing group; they blocked his path. "Look, I'll give you a nickel if you just let me go on home. My old lady's gonna be mad. She's got supper ready."

It was the wrong appeal and he knew it instantly. His tormentors moved closer with a different look in their dark eyes. "You got money? Let's see how much money you got, boy."

Juarez felt a familiar heat rising up his neck to his ears. "You ain't gonna see nothin'. You want a nickel, just let me pass."

The tallest of the three boys grabbed for Pedro's pockets. When he resisted, he found himself in a stranglehold. "Give me your money and I won't hurtch ya. Come on, fork it over."

Juarez clenched his fist. The heat in his brain seared. He threw a punch right into the crotch of the boy who had him in the headlock. He loosened his grip. Pedro shoved him away. The Negro boy's hands went down between his legs, rubbing frantically, trying to soothe his bruised testicles. Pedro tripped and fell backwards on the gravel surface. Catching himself with both hands, he felt the stones cut into the skin on his palms. The other two boys were moving in on him as he looked at the bloody scrapes on his hands. Pedro grabbed a stone and scrambled to his feet.

One of the attackers came forward. On seeing the stone in Pedro's hand, he reversed his movement. The boy made a quick turn and ran. Juarez threw the stone. It careened off the boy's skull, bounced off a nearby building to settle again on the ground. The assaulted boy began rubbing his head with a fast-moving hand, trying to ease the pain in the rising knot on his head. Feet that had been sprinting now circled in a skipping motion, his legs and arms dancing. The third and smallest boy turned and ran. He turned a corner of the alley and scaled a clap-board fence.

Pedro wiped the blood from his hands on his shirt as he ran, gasping for breath and trying to put distance between him and the Negro boys. After five blocks, Pedro figured he was safe. He paused to lean on a stone wall and tried to catch his breath. He put both of his bloody hands on the wall and pressed hard, trying to drill himself into the concrete structure. It calmed him.

OK, so they think I'm a nigger like them. Pedro felt the heat dissipate as he pressed against the cool stones of the wall. *They don't like me and whites don't like me either. They ain't getting' my money. I worked for it and it's mine. I ain't no nigger. I'm a Mexican.*

He went home up the stairs into their flat; his mother stood by the stove, a big spoon swirling in a scented stew. He sat by the window and looked out on the street, and watched the people moving there. *I'm gonna get out of here, and never come back, never come back.*

~~~~~~~~~~~~~~

Memories were flooding Pedro Juarez's mind as he walked point on the patrol; he struggled to stay focused. It helped to think about his new life as a U.S. Marine. The

Corps had become his home and his salvation. He dropped to a knee, cautiously eyeing a rise up ahead. He was looking for movement on either side of the trail.

Watch out, don't go over the next rise, wait, go to that tree put your head up there where it cuts across the horizon: Hard to see you there, don't give 'em a chance to cut you down.

I am Pedro Juarez, he reminded himself. *I'm a United States Marine, Spanish, Aztec. This is my salvation. Whatever happens this is my home now. Right now I'm doing what I was trained to do. I don't bitch about it, it's where I belong.*

He raised his clenched fist to stop the patrol. A movement to his front caught his eye. A wild fowl flew out of the brush. He called the lieutenant forward and requested they halt for a moment. The lieutenant, drenched with sweat, seemed relieved to rest and gave his permission. Juarez sat and adjusted his gear.

His mind drifted briefly to his furlough after he'd finished basic training. He was home, where he didn't want to be.

He left after two days. His thoughts plagued him as he headed to the train station and back to the base. *Don't want to be here. Want to get away from here. Whites watching me, yeah, look at me, I'm a Marine. Hold your head up, nigger; you're a Marine. Yeah gotta get outta this place, born here, so what, God damn I'll be better than these freaks, you watch me. Don't give a shit. Two days home, lost, don't belong here anymore. Same as before, roam around lonely. Gotta get the hell outta here.*

"Hey, Marine, I got something for ya."

"Go screw yourself." Pedro waved off the prostitute and picked up his pace towards the train station. He had seven days left on his leave. He decided to return to his base.

He moved faster down the street.

Train, got my ticket, trains are slow. The ones hauling supplies for the military got priority. Probably take two days to get there. Try to find a place to stay, new base Jacksonville North Carolina Camp LeJeune. Gonna be hard to find a place to hang out before I have to go back. Skin tone a problem, heard blacks not welcome there. They don't give a shit if you're not Negroid, color means everything. Fuck 'em; if I have to I'll go back on base.

For the first time in his young life, Juarez had the option to do something like that and he owed it all to the Marine Corps. They took him off the street because he could read and write. There was no question about his color or ancestry. The recruiting sergeant looked at him a little strange but there was no denying Pedro Juarez could read and write. That meant Pedro Juarez had enough brains to become a Marine. There was no question.

On the train, he met a skinny soldier who invited him to play cards. Pedro could tell the man was a Texan by the thick drawl. Pedro sat down next to the man and sized him up while he waited for the shuffle. *This guy is Texas all the way, Pedro decided. Wouldn't even talk to me in his home town. Maybe I'm just another greaser to him but the big equalizer is the uniform. He's wearing an armored division patch and I'm a Marine. That makes us fighting men and that means we're equal. Might have to save his ass someday...or the other way around.*

Juarez smiled at the thought, shook his head and motioned the patrol to move up behind him.

The Boys from Brooklyn

From his position at the rear of the patrol, Drago watched the lieutenant as he conferred with Juarez on point and then motioned for the others to follow him. *Officers move different than enlisted guys*, he thought. *Officers kinda stomp along and enlisted men stride. Must have something to do with the training.*

The patrol emerged from the jungle and headed up a trail that lead them onto a flat grassy plain. Drago noticed for the first time how dark it was in the jungle. The thick growth made them claustrophobic, and made their pace slower them they expected.

Out of our element being in the bush, Drago speculated. *Americans ain't comfortable in jungles. It's unknown, unfamiliar territory. We're used to open land, farms, woods, even swamps back home. A jungle is different. It's scary, claustrophobic and dark. Figures we'd wind up fighting in it.*

Up ahead of him, Drago saw the two college boys from Brooklyn step into the sunlight. They were gabbing as usual; probably bitching about the Marine Corps. Both of those guys were drafted and they rarely let anyone forget about that. Drago couldn't understand why they'd volunteered for the patrol. It was certainly out of character for them unless they were just out here looking for war souvenirs. Neither of those guys was happy being in the Marines and they never wanted to lend a hand with anything much.

The spindly, dark-skinned Syrian controlled the conversation as he always did. The second one, chunky and smaller, took his cues from him and parroted every statement he made. The stocky boy bolstered the Syrian's comments by laughing when he did not understand his meanings; at other times he would come up with some minor comment irrelevant to the Syrian's remarks.

They were caught in a totally masculine environment to which they could not adjust. They did not care to assimilate into that setting. Their means of coping was a not-so-subtle castigation of those around them. Drago was their target that day.

Drago remembered his last encounter with the two college boys when he asked them to help him pull the breech-block off one of the 90mm antiaircraft guns. The breech-block was heavy and hard to lift out of its fittings. One of the guys was of Syrian extraction and had discovered after only a short time in the outfit that Corporal Stoyon was Hungarian.

"The Hunky here is obviously in a situation that has challenged his intellect," the Syrian replied as they stood around the gun mount. "He's reached the point where the task is at variance with his ability to think it through."

"We should give the little fellow a hand," the Syrian's buddy indicated. They pulled the block and set it on the gun carriage.

I should never have asked these assholes for a hand, Drago thought as he went to work on the block with a clean cloth. *I should have hauled my balls up to my ears straining to lift this thing before I asked them to help. They're just gonna stand there and bullshit while I work. What is it with them? Both of 'em are educated enough to be officers.*

Drago was in no mood for either of them on that day. He was remembering the night before at the slop-chute. Just then he hated anyone who lived anywhere near Brooklyn, much less in it. He'd been drinking beer with

Charlie the Italian from 4th Avenue and Nevins Street in the heart of Brooklyn. As usual, when Drago and Charlie got drunk they heckled each other; just enjoying the time off and pounding down the beers. They left the slop-chute around 2100 and started back for the tent area. The walk sobered Drago up and he began to look around at the jungle that grew thick on each side of the trail. There were still Japanese out there, and they were in no shape to deal with them. *What if one of them renegades grabbed ya while you're soused?* Drago was sobering up quickly and walking a little faster. *What the hell ya gonna do all juiced up? You wouldn't stand a chance.* Charlie stopped suddenly and pointed up the trail where they could see the bright headlights of a vehicle approaching. The lights were sweeping up, down, right and left like a beacon in the black night.

"Douse them fuckin' lights!" Charlie yelled and started striding up the road "Ya son a bitches, put out them fuckin' lights." The Jeep maintained its speed, heading straight towards them. Charlie planted himself directly in the center of the road and held up a hand to halt the oncoming vehicle.

There was no stopping Charlie, who headed for the Jeep and never made a move to avoid an imminent collision. Drago chased after him realizing that in his condition Charlie had more balls than brains. "Charlie, get the hell off the road! They ain't gonna stop!"

Charlie halted with his hands on his hips and glared at the oncoming vehicle. "The hell they won't. Them bastards will stop, or I'll make 'em stop...shut off them fuckin' lights!"

As Drago dropped a shoulder and pushed the crazy Guinea off the road, there was a screech of brakes and the

Jeep swerved to get past them without running anybody over. That's when Drago noticed it was a Jeep full of officers.

Charlie didn't notice the occupants. He scrambled to his feet and shouted at the passing vehicle. "I told you assholes to turn off them fuckin' lights, didn't I?"

The Jeep's brake lights illuminated and Drago saw two men looking back in their direction. Despite the dark jungle trail, he recognized the passengers and popped to attention giving Charlie a painful elbow in the ribs. The battalion commander, a major, and his executive officer, a captain, were sitting in the Jeep. The captain driving stopped and backed up the Jeep to where Drago and Charlie were standing. The captain got out of the Jeep and faced the two drunks.

"What's your name, Marine?" The Executive Officer asked, pointing a finger at Charlie.

Charlie was still a little shaky on his feet but magaged to stand at something that vaguely resembled the position of attention. "PFC Charles Conjoles, sir!"

Drago was fighting a grin and thinking how quickly Charlie sobered up in this situation. *Funny how the military stuff kicks ya in the ass when ya run into an officer,* he mused. *All that bullshit in boot camp pays off when the chips are down.*

"And yours, Mister?" The executive officer turned to Drago.

"Corporal Drago Stoyon, sir."

The captain climbed back into the Jeep and looked at his commanding officer. The major was too drunk to care much. He usually was. Drago had never seen him without a forlorn look on his face and at least a couple of drinks under his belt. Maybe the officers were too drunk to remember much about this incident. If they did remember, he was bound to miss out on a third stripe. Charlie didn't give a shit. He was about to rotate home and there was little they could do to him in the time he had left on Guam. The captain seemed to be wondering how to end the encounter as Drago stood looking at the drunken major in the Jeep. The guy was a sad case. *What makes him that way*, Drago wondered. *Maybe he screwed up during the war and got a lot of guys killed. It's gotta be hard on the captain having to take orders from a lush like that.*

In contrast to the slumping senior officer, Drago noted the captain looked trim and in control despite the booze he could smell on the man's breath. He had a snoot as full as the major's but he still had that officer bearing; he was still in control of the situation.

"Consider yourselves on report, and consider yourselves lucky that's all it is...for now." The Jeep roared off in a spray of dust. No sooner had the Jeep departed than Charlie roared with laughter. Drago thought the Jeep would stop again, but it kept going. "Easy Charlie fer Christ sakes, they'll hear ya. Ain't we enough trouble as it is? Holy shit, I wonder what he means we're on report. At least he didn't say we had to report. Jesus Charlie what's so funny?" Charlie stopped laughing long enough to answer Drago "Didn't ya see the stupid look on the Major's face? I thought he was gonna cry. Jesus that was funny. We'll probably be buck-ass privates again; that's the way it looks. Fuck 'em. I don't give a damn: it was worth it to see the look on his face."

That's the way of things in the Marine Corps, he was thinking as they walked. *Ya fuck up, ya gotta pay. Only question is whether it will be a deck court or a full summary court-martial. Ain't no chance at sergeant now and they might just take the two stripes I got. Just my luck getting' wound up with this dumb Guinea tonight. That's some tough shit. Ya fuck up, ya gotta pay.*

Drago headed for his tent worrying about losing his rank over a drunken stunt and promising to steer clear of guys from Brooklyn in future. *I've got two years to go out here*, he thought, feeling like a condemned prisoner. *I can't go home with nothin' to show for it. I can just hear the old man laughin' at me if I don't get somewhere in the service. Goddamn that Guinea bastard; you pick your friends to stand with and you have to fall with them when shit happens.*

The next morning, Cpl. Stoyon's name had been removed from the eligibility list for the sergeant's test. He was disappointed but oddly reassured about his assessment of the captain. Stoyon had to give the man credit. Drunk as he was, he remembered their names. He decided the Battalion Executive Officer was a good man, a good officer worth respect. There was no sense blaming Charlie Conjoles. He was just a guy from Brooklyn like the two shitbirds watching him work on the breech-block.

"Maybe we should help the little fellow," said the Syrian as he slumped down on a sandbag and lit a smoke.

"Up yours." Drago sneered and concentrated on his work.

"Hey, Harvey," the Syrian said. "Do you think he finished the seventh grade?"

"Maybe," Harvey said from another sandbag seat on the other side of the gun pit. "But that would be unusual for a Hunky. They usually die off before they get that far in school. It's the percentages, you know."

Drago left the breech-block looking for the can of gasoline they'd brought to soak through the grease. The Syrian grabbed Grago's elbow as he passed; he spun to face his tormentor with an angry glare. "You can bullshit all you want, but keep your fuckin' hands off me."

"The Hunky gets mad, does he?"

"Go fuck yourself. I'm in no mood for your shit today."

"What's the matter, Hunky? Did I hurt your feelings?"

"Listen, asshole...You and your shit-bird friend there, all you do is mock people. You got some idea that going to college makes you above the rest of us. You think you're the only ones with brains around here, but that's bullshit. Better men than you are flushed down the toilet every day."

Drago tried to shove by the man, amazed that he'd been able to keep from throwing a punch for this long. The college boy from Brooklyn stepped in to block his patch. "Get out of my way before I knock you on your ass!"

The college boy reached for him as his buddy came from around the gun pit looking to get in on the action. Drago spun away and faced them both with his fists balled at his sides. "Don't do it! Just don't fucking do it! Either one of you ever touches me again, I'll kill ya!"

There was something in Drago's blazing stare that told the two college boys from Brooklyn they were treading dangerous waters. They were not willing to fight but they were also not willing to suffer a damaging blow to their egos. Drago had seen that kind of crap before in and out of the Marine Corps.

"This asshole can't take a joke," the Syrian said to Harvey. "Let's just leave him to his dirty work." They started to stroll away from the gun but Drago had more to say.

"There's another thing you two turds need to get straight. I'm a corporal in the Marines. I don't give a shit how you address anyone else here, but you don't ever call me anything but Corporal Stoyon."

The two college boys from Brooklyn just grinned and moved away. Drago heard one of them mumble something disrespectful but that wasn't important now. He had these guys. They pushed it and he confronted them. They backed down and that meant they wouldn't try it again, at least not to his face. That was the first item of good news on that bad day when he lost another a shot at sergeant. The other item was Drago Stoyon's realization that he could control his capacity to kill.

The Water Buffalo

Drago froze just as he was about to emerge from the jungle onto a sunlit plain. A shadow to his rear, caught by acute peripheral vision, disappeared into the mass of vegetation. He turned, scanned the area of the blur. Another sighting to the left of the first detained him. He held his position while the rest of the patrol moved forward.

He brought up his rifle ready to fire, sighting in he scanned the area to his rear. He set an ark one hundred and eighty degree, and swept it three times. There was nothing he could discern in the area they just covered, but he was uneasy

Pay attention to what you're doing, fer Christ sakes! he warned himself. *Your mind is travelling too much. Hear that noise. Hear it. Look around. Be careful, movement, be alert. You're just as bad as those jerks horsin' around, keep your mind on your work.*

He turned and watched as Juarez moved into the high grass; the men followed detouring past a nest of hornets that blocked their path. Drago correlated their movement with that of the renegades they were hunting.

If the Japs are out there, they're doing the same thing, circling around us.

He imagined a few of the renegades in his mind, slipping around the clumsy Marine patrol, laughing all the way.

Yeah, they're halfway across the island by now.

He grew angry, not because they could not make contact, but disturbed by the cavalier attitude of the

Marines with him. His image of the laughing renegades mocked him.

A trail cut through the high grass. The plain of grasses circled the jungle for 300 yards in all directions. Briars on the perimeter made a form of concertina wire, separating the tall grass from the thick vegetation. A breaching of the briars created a ripping sound, as two huge water buffalo came thundering down the trail at the Marines. They roared forward, spraying briars as they came. Their huge horns carried wreaths of thorns as they tore down the path.

Juarez quickly shifted off the path and into the grasses, then went down on one knee into kneeling position, ready to fire. The lieutenant, still on the path, went down on one knee and raised his carbine. Destruction imminent, he finally jumped off the trail into the tall grass in time to save himself from being trampled.

Drago watched as Marines went flying with a rapidity that amazed him. Rifles flew in one direction and Marines in another, all avoiding disaster by mini-seconds. The buffalo bore down on him. Their thundering hooves transfixed the corporal.

A ton at least, each one must weigh a ton or better. Move. Move—they're here!

Drago dove behind a thick teak tree as they roared towards him; he heard a violent thump and felt the tree shake as one of their horns tore into it. When they disappeared into the bush Drago inspected the tree trunk and saw a three-inch gash in the hardwood where the horns made a deep cut.

The buffalo passed; no Marines were injured, except for pride. They reassembled.

That was close. Just think what those horns could have done to you. They could have torn you in half, thought the corporal. *All that training lay back there in your mind, the need for instantaneous response shelved for months; when needed it showed up, thank God! That and a little luck saved me.*

He reached back and found that one element other than luck that could be his savior: training. He was pleased. Drago felt a little bit better about his chances with the screwed up patrol.

The Cave

On the other side of the clearing, they left the kunai grass and moved into the jungle again. There was a trail that ran parallel to a stream; it had been used. Smoothed out clay along the bed of the river betrayed the cagy renegades' attempt to cover their tracks.

With that discovery, all the men became more alert.

Juarez, still leading slowed his pace. He would move forward about a hundred yards, stop, and signal the others to halt. Juarez motioned for quiet and studied the terrain to his front. Rushing water in the stream caused any sound of movement by the renegades to be muted, causing Juarez to be cautious to the extreme. When sure of no danger he gave the signal to resume the march. Everyone was being cautious and walking more like Marines. Even P.T. O'Rielly was alert and keeping his head swiveling as they moved forward. During one of these halts, Juarez stopped and called the lieutenant forward. Drago watched as Juarez pointed to a spot to his right above the stream. Drago told the Guinea from Brooklyn to watch the rear, and went forward to see what prompted the halt. He walked up to Juarez.

"Hey, what's up?" asked Drago.

The lieutenant was moving forward to inspect the high ground above the stream.

"I told the lieutenant about the cave." Juarez answered.

"What cave?"

"The one over there; he's looking at it now. I told him we better stop and deploy, and find out if there's anyone in there. Instead he says he's going to take a look. If there's Japs in there that fuckin' guy is gonna get killed. That's no way to do it. We should deploy around it, set up a fire pattern and blast the shit outta it. Maybe chuck a grenade in there. It's kinda high; you would have to make sure the grenade gets up there. Not the way he's goin' at it." Drago nodded his affirmation.

"All dead, all dead, they'd fire and pick us off like flies on honey." Drago summed it up. "If there's anyone up there we're finished."

Juarez looked at Drago, and said. "Well, if it was to happen it should have happened already."

The lieutenant, after scouting the opening, came down and called the patrol together.

Drago paused, then said, "Let's join 'em." They went forward to the cave opening

"Nothing up there," Lieutenant Cantone said, "Let's move further up this side of the stream and see if we can make contact along the way."

Juarez led, the patrol followed. Drago fell behind. He wished to reconnoiter the cave to his own satisfaction.

Let me take a look. I'll get a grenade out and listen; if I hear anything at all I'll throw a grenade into the cave, he said to himself.

He let the patrol get ahead and sat off to the side of the opening; there he waited. The patrol moved out quickly. Drago heard nothing, eyed the cave wearily, then picked up his pace to catch up.

Juarez stopped the patrol 100 yards up river from the cave. Something caught his eye; he sent word back for Drago to come forward. When Drago approached Juarez pointed to the path to his front.

"Get a load of this," he said to Drago. "Look at the ground here and tell me what you think."

Cpl. Stoyon surveyed the area. "Sure looks like someone's been here, the ground is all flattened out. No boot prints but some indentations...look to be imprints of bare feet. I'll bet they come here for water, it looks drinkable."

"Yeah, that's what I thought," said Corporal Juarez. "I'm gonna tell the lieutenant we should deploy here. We sure as hell ain't gonna go back tonight. If we lay in an ambush maybe we'll catch 'em off guard. They might come down this evening for water; that stuff looks drinkable. You wanna tell the lieutenant?"

Given Drago was senior to him, the option to approach the lieutenant in the matter of the deployment pleased him.

"Nah, if I tell him anything, he won't listen. He's got his balls in an uproar about me for some reason, no sense in pissin' him off further. He'll listen to you; get it done." Drago said, and walked away.

Juarez called the lieutenant, and explained the situation.

"We'll deploy here," Lieutenant Cantone told the patrol. And then to Juarez he said, "Do it."

P.T., Jeremy, Tom, Juarez and Drago grouped together. Before they sat, Drago called Juarez to his side and showed him a freshly-broken branch.

"We're gonna have to be careful here tonight." Drago's voice showed concern.

K rations were the fare: cheese and crackers, a chocolate bar, a bar of dried raisins, concentrated, explosive in the digestive tract, filling. P.T. had his canteen filled with beer, Tom's with raisin jack; the rest had water. Cpl. Stoyon watched the water flow in the stream, and was surprised to see how clear it was; good for drinking, he was sure. He went down to the water, ran his hand under the flow, then cupped his hand and splashed it onto his face, felt its coolness.

The Lieutenants

The lieutenant was engaged in conversation with the Syrian. It was a long time since the corporal had any contact with Lt. Cantone. Drago's position as senior over privates was ignored by Cantone. He was told to stand a post that generally was given to those of lesser rank. At the time, Stoyon was listed for promotion to sergeant. The lieutenant knew this, and still delegated the walking post to him. He wound up walking a post like a buck ass private. Stoyon felt slighted; it was considered a reprimand. Drago did not understand why he was singled out.

A spark was ignited when the lieutenant made overtures to the two sergeants, Perlas and Braxton, seeking recognition and association; they ignored Lt. Cantone. He knew the two sergeants ran the battalion; any semblance of stature in the chain of command through association was denied him. The sergeants by demanding full military courtesy in their contact with the lieutenant let him understand his place as well as theirs. A curt salute and minimal recognition gave notice to Cantone of his position in the strata of command.

Watching Stoyon with Perlas and Braxton, and seeing the lack of formality generated among that fraternity galled the lieutenant.

Another run in with Cantone occurred on maneuvers. During the placement of the 90 millimeter antiaircraft gun, the battalion armor, it became a challenge to each crew to see who would finish setting the gun down in position for firing first. Drago made a bet with Perlas that his people would have their gun ready for firing before his crew. Drago learned fast, and threw in a few innovations of his own after reading the manuals on the 90s. He knew that setting the gun down on the ground with a pitch over ten degrees would keep the weapon locked into the carriage and nearly impossible to remove for emplacement in firing position. It prevented the carriage from breaking away from the body of the weapon. You needed flat ground where the body of the weapon could easily be pulled off the road carriage and quickly assembled into firing position.

"But sir, ya can't set the gun down there; the pitch is over ten degrees," Drago said to Lt. Cantone.

It was getting dark. Preparing the gun for firing during the day was tough enough; at night it would be a trial Drago did not want to face.

Cantone was having no argument. "Set the gun down where I told you, Corporal." The response was curt.

He accentuated the rank, defining Drago's position. Drago had to obey, and knew he would be out the five dollars he bet Perlas, as well as a bit of pride.

The first attempt at getting the gun off the carriage almost ended in disaster, the tons of metal tipped precariously. Perlas watched as a second attempt was made to disengage the carriage from the bulk of the cannon, again wasted energy by the frustrated crew.

Perlas and his crew sat silently on their gun's platform, gazing unbelievably at Cpl. Stoyon's crews thwarted attempts to disengage the weapon. The corporal had bested them in the exercise many times before. 1st Lt. Warren and Sgt. Braxton joined Perlas; they all watched the maddening effort.

Drago's crew brought the gun back to its original position, engaged with the carriage. The crew, exhausted, fell on the piece at various points, sweating and panting.

Braxton approached Drago.

"What's up, kid?"

"Oh Jesus, Sarge, I told that lieutenant, that Cantone, ya couldn't set the piece down here because of the pitch. Take a look, it's over ten degrees, the freakin' thing ain't gonna break."

"I got ya. Sit tight, I'll get back to you."

Braxton went back to Lt. Warren and Perlas, spoke a few words to Warren, then moved off to find Cantone. Five minutes later Braxton came back to the crew.

"Okay, move it. Find a good flat place and put it down."

Nothing more was said. The crew went into action; within fifteen minutes they all sat down on the platforms outriggers, the cannon ready to fire. Drago wondered why the Marine Corps tolerated officers like Lt. Cantone when they had good men like Lt. Warren.

~~~~~~~~~~~~~~~

The tall Alabamian 1st Lt. Warren, hulking and brash, had a body that reflected his hard-working Alabama roots. Under the decorum of Marine tans lay a swamp-sinner, part man, part boy. Presented with the Navy Cross, Silver Star with two oak leaf clusters, a Bronze Star, and five combat commendations; he was known as Madcap Warren, Attack-Happy Warren.

"Is that all you know, Mister?" His instructor in combat maneuvers asked.

"As long as I lead the attack; yeah, that's right." He was all man on the line with his Marines.

When Warren's rifle misfired in combat, he grabbed the barrel and swung it like a club. The Japanese soldier's collar bone, hip, and cheek bones were crushed. Another time, a machinegun barking, slicing the terrain, Marines crying out, Warren went forward emptying his sidearm, reloading, attack, attack, gripping yellow-skinned man's Adam's apple and thrashing him back and forth, tearing out his larynx. The body was thrown away as a child would a toy. With the other hand, his fist smashed into the second gunner, sending him up and over the rim of the emplacement.

On another occasion, Warren enraged, a gin bottle in hand, gripped around the neck; stupor-controlling, emblazoned, the officer's club a shambles, torn and destroyed by the offended Warren. Six officers of various ranks were unnerved by the ferocity of the attack. The officer, saying the words "White trash," lay bleeding at the far end of the destroyed Quonset.

Warren, seeing Lt. Canton's back to him as he entered the headquarters tent that evening, singled out his rump and let fly an extremely large boot, catching him square on the ass. Cantone, with mouth open, his anus cleaved, and burning with pain, with flesh forced on bone, looked at his senior in command, and dared not question the brazen assault. First Lt. Warren walked around the man with the pained expression, and went out the far end of the tent.

~~~~~~~~~~~~~~~

Drago didn't see any of that, but he knew that Warren had saved him and his gun crew a lot of trouble. It was worth losing five bucks if you could work with a guy like Lt. Warren.

Drago liked Warren, and wished he could deal with him all the time instead of the disgruntled Cantone.

Night Deployment

Juarez and Stoyon took in hand the deployment of the troops. McVey and Stoyon would hold the center, facing the stream. To his right with the Guinea from Brooklyn would be Juarez, P. T. and Tom would be to Stoyon's left. Further to their left the college boys and the lieutenant held the flank. Stoyon called them all together.

"Now listen, make sure where your front is at all times. Don't move around. You don't want to be disoriented. Any questions? Okay, let's take our positions."

Drago's tone left no doubt as to who was in charge. The lieutenant made no comment. It would be easy to blame the corporal if there was a screw up.

Darkness flooded in on them, as did swarms of mosquitoes and gnats. It became a plague, a total infestation. Welts were in abundance. Bloodied bodies of mosquitoes were left on skin, as the need to destroy others became the prime objective. It lasted one hour; as fast as they came, they left leaving itchy red welts to remind the Marines they were in a hostile environment where nearly anything could hurt you or kill you.

It was a fifty-fifty deal. Each group selected which of their partners would sleep and which would take the first watch. McVey and Stoyon set their backs to a hardwood tree. Their shoulders touched, as much for security as for knowledge of where the other was. McVey requested the first watch.

No moon to illuminate, no moon to afford them the luxury of tracking movement. The night became their enemy, their ears their comrades. Sound was the only ally. They scrutinized with their senses. Pebbles moved in the creek bed, vacillating between thunder and blissful quiet. All sounds were contorted. Fear, charged adrenaline, and frayed nervous systems were taunted by the simplest motion. The situation did not sit well with the corporal. He never cared for the inaction they had to endure that evening. On Iwo Jima during the battle, the confusion combined with the totality of the engagement took its toll on the individual; still, he felt better there than in the situation he was in now.

Drago slept restlessly, a nagging, floating in and out of slumber. After two hours he woke and gave McVey a poke with his elbow, startling him.

"What's up, everything okay?"

"It's okay, nothin' goin' on, relax. I just wanted to let you know it's your time to try to sleep."

"Okay, Okay, I got ya, it's my time to sleep. Yeah, thanks, Drago."

McVey knew he dozed off and was embarrassed by his lapse. Drago knew, but said nothing to him.

Each man was left to his thoughts. P.T.'s mind drifted to the incursion by the water buffalo. They were all unnerved, all laughing to cover up their foolishness. Lt. Cantone became angry with P.T. for laughing, told him to act like a Marine. P.T. just smiled and handed the officer the rifle he discarded during the incident. The lieutenant went away quietly.

All quiet now, P.T. surmised, *two flying beasts made soldiers out of a bunch of boys. Guys are all military now, training taking over, yeah.*

Tom grabbed P.T.'s arm. "Ya hear that? Something's moving down there."

"Naw," said P.T. "It's just the steam; that's rocks movin'."

"No, it's somethin' else. Listen."

P.T. strained to hear.

"Ya might be right; I think there is something down there. It's like someone splashing, walkin' on water. Maybe it's Jesus H. Christ, ya dumb ass."

Tom snickered, and sat back. "Yeah, think you're smart, don't ya."

At about the same time, McVey and Drago were trying to rid themselves of ants that had quietly infiltrated their person, crawling up their sleeves, pant legs, and underneath their utility shirts. When the ants made their parade to their satisfaction, they started to bite. Fire ants gouge, you bleed, they bled. They had no idea what was attacking them, they knew they were being attacked.

"Jesus Christ all mighty!" Drago said, while trying to keep his voice down. McVey jumped up and out of position, dropping his rifle as he did, freeing his hands to counter the attack. Each time he grabbed an ant, it stuck to his fingers and clung there, biting. He had to take his hands and rub them on the ground to free them of the marauders; they clung there tenaciously.

The two Marines were furious. When they needed to be alert, they had to contend with the ants. Minutes passed before they rid themselves of the annoying raiders. They nursed their welts, and settled down.

Tom again heard a rustling sound going on to his right; it further unnerved him. He told P.T. "I'm gonna fire, there's something out there."

"Don't do it," P.T warned Tom. "You fire and everyone else breaks loose; who knows what will happen."

Tom raised the Thompson machinegun. He released the safety. P.T. grabbed the barrel at the same time Tom fired, and sent a five round burst into the darkness.

"What the fuck was that?" Drago said aloud, "Jeremy, get down get down!"

Jeremy quickly threw his body to the earth. Drago was already sprawled on the ground, trying to bury himself.

No fox hole, no fox hole. Should have dug one, all should have! My fault, didn't instruct. Drago scolded himself.

One more report, this time by an M1. A moment's pause, then hell's doors opened, firing came from all directions. The entire ambush line opened up; the dark was driven back by the flash of muzzle pumping rounds out at something, anything that might—or might not—be out there along the stream.

Drago didn't fire. He was hugging the damp jungle floor and remembering the last time he was under fire.

It happened on Iwo. Pvt. Stoyon, pinned down, firing coming at him from everywhere. He remembered hollering, "Holy shit, I'm gonna die! Stop it, stop it! I'm gonna fuckin' die!"

He prayed, as shells and bullets scattered around him. He mumbled, he prayed, he cursed, alternately blaming God and the Japanese, then pleaded with both to end the fusillade. The firing stopped. He dove for cover. The Japanese, seeing his movement, fired. Dirt and stone flew around him. Finally he rested behind a mound of dirt. Sitting there, he cursed, then laughed, for he never prayed.

The firing at the creek bed stopped. No one moved. All were petrified; any movement would get them killed. The silence from then on was eerie.

The Scream

The moon appeared between grey, full clouds. The stream could now be seen. Moon-reflected light illuminated the noise-producing pebbles.

Drago and McVey sat again at the base of the tree. The stinging of the ants was sublimated by fear caused by the barrage. A little peace settled on the patrol as the moon gave them sight.

Then, out of the jungle came a scream, a piercing scream, an anguished shriek, a scream designed to put the fear of God into the Marines. The pitch was high and penetrating.

Is it one of ours? wondered Drago. *No, it's too far away; fuckers trying to scare us. It's got to be a Jap.*

McVey grabbed onto Drago's arm; neither man said a word. P.T. took a long drink from his canteen of beer; he wished he had a stronger mixture to chase away the prevailing terror. Tom guzzled the raisin jack, and cursed that it did nothing to suppress the fit of shaking that racked his body. Both Brooklyn college boys excreted bodily fluids. The Guinea from Brooklyn had a flashback of the night he and his sister had taken a beating from their father for sassing him. The scream heard was the same as those emitted from his sister as she cowered at the hands of their father. He drew his legs up to his chest, curling into a ball.

Dawn broke; with it came relief. They all gathered around the stream. They laughed, horsed around, prodded and playfully patted each other on their backs. No one was injured. The scream, the incursion of the enemy as is always the case, settled into the subconscious of the participants. No one mentioned it.

The lieutenant was not amused he confronted the men in the patrol. "Who fired the first shots?" he asked,

Drago knew the one responsible was either Tom or the Guinea from Brooklyn, it was a Thompson that fired, and they had them. They were not about to offer an explanation. But Drago also understood the lieutenant. If Drago said that he fired the first shot, there could be no reprimand. Drago's experience in combat forbade retaliation from a non-combatant. Cantone, just out of officer candidate school in the states, had no combat experience.

"I did," said Stoyon

"You did? You did, why?"

"I thought I heard something out there."

The lieutenant moved toward Drago. He was infuriated with the corporal; he also knew it was a Thompson that fired and that Drago could not have been the one who fired. Saying that he let go the first salvo was just another attempt by the corporal to subvert his authority. It was another symbol of their strained relationship. He faced off with the corporal; the corporal did not move as Cantone pressed forward. A fit of rage engulfed the lieutenant; spastically, with flailing arms he confronted the stern-faced Croat. Speaking in a garbled profusion of syllabic nonsense no one could understand, he tried to undo the damage the confrontation produced, throwing his arms in the air he walked off, mumbling.

The corporal and the lieutenant had to share the blame of putting the mundane before duty.

Drago crossed over the stream, and looked over the area where they noticed the trodden earth on the previous day. He checked the area again; a footprint was now visible that he believed did not exist previously. Brushing past some foliage, a red stain appeared on his sleeve, a light pinkish blotch spread there.

*Could it be?*he thought, *could one of them have come down here last night? Maybe they were right to fire. Why would any one of them come down here for water? They knew we were here—or did they?*

The risk involved should have deterred them. Drago came to the conclusion the renegades had balls, and wished to challenge the "nation's finest."

The patrol moved through the jungle more alert.

Mosquitoes and gnats again tormented. They were less of a problem, a secondary annoyance now. The barrage and the scream of the previous evening imbedded in their minds controlled their actions.

Juarez leading, extremely cautious now, leaving nothing to chance, scanned the jungle thoroughly. They pushed deeper into the green wall of vines and creepers.

The Battleground

They came upon an open field. It was pock-marked with shell holes. Torn away trees and high grasses gave way to new greenery. For 200 yards, wave upon wave of new grass covered the scene of the last battle on Guam. Towards the far end of the field from where the patrol came out of the jungle were thatched roofs standing on severed palm trees. The structures were mostly burned and leveled by what looked like artillery fire. Most of the trees out in the clearing had been blasted into splintered stumps in a half-circle of makeshift buildings. It was the last stronghold of Japanese resistance on the island.

Juarez stood conferring with the lieutenant. The patrol on the perimeter of the jungle waited for instructions. Drago worked his way up to them. Juarez immediately engaged Stoyon in the conference.

"We had better take care out there." He spoke directly to Drago.

Drago took a knee, leaned on his rifle and stared at the open space.

"Best to form a skirmish line while going through this area," Drago interjected. "I guess spreading them about ten yards apart should do it. There might be dangerous shit out there, some stuff left behind after the battle."

The lieutenant didn't acknowledge Drago's advice. Juarez said he needed more time to check out the place before he brought out the patrol. The corporal and the lieutenant nodded their assent. Juarez took time to reconnoiter the open terrain to his front, surveying from side to side where the open space met the jungle. Juarez alone moved out into the pock-marked terrain.

"If there's anyone there, he's going to draw fire. We have to be ready to cover him." Drago addressed the lieutenant.

The lieutenant glared at Drago. The corporal noted the disdain; he also noted the stupidity of it. When all their attention should be on getting the job done without any problems, he had to contend with the man's animosity. He wished he could rap a clenched fist on the lieutenant's head and say, "Wake up, jarhead; there is work to be done." The lieutenant made no move to alert the men watching Juarez from the edge of the jungle. Drago would have to do that.

He ignored the lieutenant and surveyed the jungle on the other side of the abandoned Japanese base camp for any motion that would give someone away. Juarez turned and pumped his arm for the patrol to move forward. Drago ordered the Marines onto the field.

He spoke to them as they moved out. "Now, as we go through here, we're going to form a skirmish line, each man separated by ten yards until we get across the field."

The Marines listened to the corporal, yet their eyes were wide looking at the area before them. They placed themselves the required distance apart and were ready to move out on command. Drago, seeing a look of perplexity on their faces, decided to add to his instructions.

"There might be some stuff ya want to pick up out there; don't touch nothin'. It might be booby-trapped"

Most of the men on the patrol wished to acquire some sort of souvenir on their mission and some went along for that purpose alone.

"Remember last night and the scream; these guys have us pegged. Ya never can tell if they fucked up somethin' out there to surprise you. Be careful. If ya see something ya want, call me and I'll look it over. Now let's go."

Juarez took a knee and stood his ground and waited for the patrol to catch up. They moved forward. P.T. was in position in the center of the line; to his right was McVey. Drago was stationed to the right of McVey. Tom was to the left of P. T.

They proceeded to a point halfway through the field, and approaching the Japanese base camp Drago noticed a swath of grass just in front of P.T., lying flat and out of place from the rest of the grasses. He surveyed a line of the flattened grasses crossing the full length of the field. Something did not seem right to him. He was about call to the patrol to a halt when he saw P.T. pull his leg as it snagged on something. P.T. thought it was a root, and tried to disengage his foot. He yanked his foot forward as hard as he could. A popping sound was heard; Stoyon knew immediately what it was. Two American-made grenades were charged, a whistling was heard, as two safety bars flew off in opposite directions.

Stoyon hollered, "Get down! Move, get down, P.T., down on the ground!"

He ran toward P.T. and McVey. P.T. looked at the corporal running towards him, and smiled. McVey seemed to understand, he threw his body forward to avoid whatever it was that Drago had detected. The blast caught McVey's flying body and propelled it high into the air. P.T. did not hear the blast; a fragment of metal had pierced his brain, entering just above his ear. He died.

Drago was thrown back by the blast. A shard of shrapnel had sliced through his upper arm. Dazed by the concussion, he heard Tom barking out orders from some far-off place.

"Get down, and stay down, don't move."

Tom felt the burst directly to his face, felt its pressure. The fragments of the grenade tore grass and air all about him, yet left him unscathed. He took command.

There was screaming all around him. Tom was surprised the howling was not coming from those affected by the blast. Tom put the thought aside, and went to P.T.'s aid. P.T. lay inert, face down in the dirt. Tom could see no marks on the Irishman; he turned him over. He inspected the man. The blood coming from his ear left no doubt of P.T.'s state. He set him down gently and then rushed to McVey.

McVey's eyes were open, pleading through the shock. Tom cradled McVey in his arms. As he held him a warm wetness invaded Tom's fatigues, and blood pulsed through his fingers where he cradled him.

"Jesus, Drago where are you? Good Christ, Good Christ!" McVey moaned and looked at Tom for help. Drago felt cool dirt on his face, and he also heard the screaming. He tried to clear his mind. The cool earth soothed, he rubbed his face on the ground.

"Jesus, Drago, where the fuck are you?"

Tom's call snapped Drago out of savoring the earth. He braced his arms on the ground to rise; a pain shot through his right arm. The pain throbbed and spread to his shoulder, and down his back. He forced the pain aside.

There is a way, he said to himself, bury it, don't submit. He jumped up, ran to where he heard Tom's plea. He looked around.

"My Christ, it's P.T. and McVey!" His right arm was immobile at his side. "Jesus, where is my rifle?

The thought of his neglect in not taking his weapon with him overshadowed all else. He ran back and picked up the rifle with his left hand. While running back to where Tom was, he chewed himself out.

No matter what happens, ya don't leave your rifle, your weapon is your savior, your guardian, you never leave a friend behind and you never leave your weapon.

Tom's eyes pleaded with Drago, "Jesus, Drago, looka McVey, looka' McVey."

"Let me see where the wound is." He noted the blood on Tom's fatigues. He helped Tom turn Jeremy over. Drago's good hand went to the small of his friend's back. It rested on raw flesh.

"Come on; let's see how bad it is."

Jeremy moaned his eyes wide with fear.

Drago surveyed the wound. *Mother of God,* he thought.

"Ya got a pad?" he asked Tom.

"What pad?"

"A pad from your first aid kit, the one that's got the sulfa packet in it."

"Yeah, yeah."

Tom ripped the first aid kit off his cartridge belt. He tried to open it with his fingers; it didn't budge.

"Take your knife and open it. Hurry up, for Christ sakes!"

Tom split it open with his blade.

"Open the packet; spread the sulfa on the wound. Now put the bandage over it and press."

"It ain't gonna fit, it's too big, the wound is too big." He whispered to Drago. "Can't stop the blood from comin' out. Holy shit Drago, what we gonna do?"

They glanced at each other, a look of desperation passed between them.

He's gonna die, thought Drago.

"Christ, we have nothin' to kill the pain," Tom moaned.

The outcome of McVey's condition Drago had witnessed on Iwo Jima. He tried to soothe McVey.

"Take it easy, you'll be all right, we're gonna get you outta here."

"Where's the fuckin' lieutenant? He's gotta know what's goin' on fer Christ sakes," Tom spit out. The sadness of the situation overwhelmed him. He turned from Drago and sighed.

"I gotta take care of myself, Tom," Drago said, and tore open the sleeve on his fatigue jacket where the shrapnel entered. He removed his first aid kit, opened it with his bayonet, tore the packet with the sulfa and spread it on the wound. With his teeth and other hand he pulled the surgical pad out of the pouch, then put the center of it on the wound and pressed; the two strips of gauze holding the pad he placed around his arm and knotted them with the aid of his teeth.

"Stay with him, Tom. I gotta see what's goin' on," he said.

He moved away and towards P.T., and bent down by his side. *What a fuckin' waste. Look at my friend. The war is over, this sort of stuff shouldn't happen. Oh, Christ, Pete, who's gonna tell Mary and your mom? You're special to them. Oh, Christ P.T., I'm gonna miss ya. Where the fuck is everybody?*

The confusion subsided; shame overcame those that called out.

Juarez again surveyed the area.

"All you guys smarten up; watch the jungle. Shoot anything that moves; I don't care what it is!" Juarez shouted.

Drago thought Juarez was right. Those that set the trap were probably watching their every move. Why they did not engage the disoriented group confused Drago.

Juarez questioned Drago, "What about P.T. and McVey?"

"P.T.'s dead, McVey's goin', he's bad off." He felt his voice breaking, he turned away from Juarez.

The corporal watched Tom stroking Jeremy's hair. He was surprised at Tom's tenderness.

Ya just can't figure out people. Tom could just as well get you killed, and then try to save your ass, he thought to himself.

McVey looked up at Tom, his eyes wide with pleading. Jeremy's body started to shake, spastic in the throes of death. Tom rocked him, holding him tightly. He died in his arms. Tom continued to rock his lifeless body.

The lieutenant appeared at the edge of the jungle; how he got there was a mystery.

As the fear of other threats waned, the patrol gathered around their dead comrades. Ponchos and rifles were gathered, and stretchers made. Drago insisted on being one of the stretcher bearers. Juarez was still on point, and the Guinea from Brooklyn the rear guard. For two excruciating hours they hauled the bodies of their comrades through the undergrowth. Exhausted, they laid the stretchers down by the road where they originally entered the jungle.

Lt. Cantone flagged down a passing jeep. He left the group there to ponder the excursion that took the life of two of their mates. They were quiet. Juarez and Drago guarded the departed and thought of the uselessness of the patrol. The war was over and two men dead—it was a bitter experience. They sat there brushing away the flies trying to feast on their friends

The corporal wondered about the spirits of the dead men. Would their souls haunt them? For the trio, Drago, Juarez and Tom, the haunting had begun; guilt saddened them. They as others before them drew the pain of responsibility for the disaster that occurred: They would handle it each in their own way.

Two trucks rolled up. The two bodies were put in one truck, the patrol in the other. Cpl. Juarez, Cpl. Stoyon, and Tom rode with the bodies.

Drago was sent to the Naval hospital. His wound was dressed there. Although it seemed to be only a flesh wound, the shrapnel had torn a muscle in his arm. Drago was told he could not leave the hospital for at least two weeks.

Vengeance consumed him; it was his duty to go out on any assignment related to bringing in the renegades. For the present he was forced to wait. He was constantly tormented by the incident.

Ya gotta stop it, he told himself, you know how it goes, ya gotta forget about the whole thing, go about your business. Marines don't dwell on such things. Remember the division when you came back from Iwo, it was as if nothing had changed. Everybody went about their job, training for the invasion of Japan. He tried to look at the disaster rationally; it was useless.

The War Criminal Stockade

A good portion of the time spent in the hospital Drago reflected on the mentality of the Japanese. Drago knew leaflets were strewn throughout the jungle, demanding full cooperation with the Americans. They were told not to resist any longer; the Emperor demanded it. Why then these renegades? The question brought to mind the war criminal stockade south of the Talofofo estuary. His battery was chosen to guard the internees. In the fall 1946 the Seabees put together a stockade. Four towers were placed at the corners of an enclosed rectangle, barbed wire topped chain link fencing. Eight back-to-back Quonsets, with twelve cubicles in each, housed 96 war criminals. There were beside the four towers eight walking posts, one on each cell block. Meshed wire windows on the doors of the cells gave the Marine guards access to the activities of the prisoners.

Four auxiliary generators were placed with attached cables inside the stockade. Four searchlights on the generators were trained on the cell blocks; these were needed for emergencies only. Tents outside of the enclosure housed the guards. Next to the tents a sheet metal overhang housed the electrical plant that supplied power to the area. Two huge generators lit up the four towers, and lights along the walking posts. Next to the overhang, another much larger tent housed about sixty witnesses, all Japanese, doing the bidding of the emperor by cooperating in the investigation of the war criminals. Not all the Japanese billeted there believed that the stature they enjoyed during their press for dominance in Asia would not come about again. The war criminals housed on Guam came from all over the South Pacific area. They were there for committing murder and other horrendous acts against their American prisoners of war and civilians in their charge.

Being overmatched during the Japanese invasion, the American garrison on Guam capitulated. Naval personnel in rather remote areas of the island, not knowing of the surrender fought on in the jungle. When captured they were immediately beheaded. Japanese officers were not held accountable to anyone for their actions regarding their treatment of prisoners. The beheading of captives was totally up to the discretion of the officer in charge.

Though the Japanese propagandized the theory of freeing the yellow man from the dominance of the Caucasians, their doctrine was negated by the total subjugation of residents of Guam by the invaders. Lashings and beheading were common for minor infractions. Control was paramount, assimilation the goal; the people of Guam had no love for the Japanese. With the Americans it was totally different. Gregarious to the extreme, they plied the population with gifts for favors either social or sexual; a good meal was as good as a piece of ass.

Senior Japanese officers were held accountable for war crimes by the victors; one of them was a Major Goto. Designated as a war criminal for the beheading of captured military personnel on Guam, his internment was the result of the horrific bombardment by the Marines in the late stages of the campaign. Stunned and immobilized by a bursting shell late in the battle, the Marines took him prisoner. Major Goto lost no time in resisting once he regained consciousness. Eight Marines were occupied in holding him down. The final result was a Marine clubbing the major with a rifle butt; it was repeated every time the major woke.

Binding was the alternative, they bound him from head to foot. Totally powerless, he frothed and strained at his bonds. The Marines left him to fester, wondering why somebody didn't kill the bastard. The major was fixated; his main objective was to commit Seppuku before the Americans overran his command. He was thwarted by the bombardment. Eventually he was brought to the stockade in a strait jacket. They removed the strait jacket with great care. All four Marines escorting the major to his new home exited with haste as another guard slammed the cell door behind them. The major, released, charged the door as the guard attempted to engage the latch closing the cell door. It took all five Marines to get it finally closed. The major frothed in desperation.

It did not end there; freed from the strait jacket, he waited for evening. As the sun set he braced both arms on the side walls of the cell and proceeded to kick out the rear panel of the cell in an attempt to escape. Alarms were sounded. Eight posted guards and twenty off-duty Marines awaken by the disturbance subdued Major Goto.

Binding prevented further attempts at escape; a straitjacket was used again to control the major. Kicking at everyone attempting to feed him became a chore, until an enterprising Marine came up with a harness that tied Goto's legs to a noose around his neck. Major Goto lost his appetite for escape after that...but not his resolve.

Feeding him was always a problem. He spit out all the food given to him. It was necessary to save the prisoner for trial and the hangman's noose. If he died due to starvation, there would be an inquiry. The Marine command wished to avoid that possibility. They brought in Yamashita Tatsuo, a witness and a former orderly of the major to feed him. The appearance of Imperil Corporal

Yamashita quieted the recalcitrant prisoner. The major ate. The guards and brass were pleased.

In general, the internees were cooperative. Two admirals from a minor post in the Pacific area were the highest ranking military personnel in the stockade. Drago and other corporals were relegated to the walking post. Their main responsibility was to make sure all of the prisoners stayed alive, that in no way they tried to harm themselves.

Closer scrutiny of the prisoners was generated by a Marine private seeking a souvenir. He gave a pencil to one of the admirals; the prisoner promised the private a drawing of a battlewagon, with his signature attached a gift he wished to display to the folks back home. The admiral took the pencil, placed the end of it against the cell wall with the point towards the center of the enclosure, and proceeded to stab himself by ramming his body into it.

The guard was again turned out in force to subdue the man and remove the pencil from the admiral's breast. The admiral sulked; his attempt at saving face had been quelled. The private was reprimanded. The stockade was again quiet.

Three weeks of duty, and the constant vigilance needed to attend to the prisoners began to take its toll on the Marines. Minor infractions by the prisoners were met with a handful of dirt poured on the offending internee's cell floor. The dirt placed there was considered a breach perpetrated by the prisoner and a flaunting of the rules. Buckets of water and tooth brushes were given to the prisoners; they were instructed to scrub down their cell floor.

Prayer and meditation occupied most of the prisoners' time. An inspection party from the army prosecutor's office came to question the prisoners about their treatment in the stockade; an interpreter was in attendance. They interviewed all the prisoners. A number of the prisoners claimed they were not treated with respect, and that their rank was ignored by the Marine guards. A communiqué was sent to battalion headquarters by the army high command. It stated the prisoner's rights had to be recognized; no cruel or inhumane punishment was to be tolerated. There could be no ramifications at the trial attesting to unjust or retaliatory action by the Marines.

The edict really pissed Perlas and Braxton off. The men were instructed to take whatever action necessary to thwart any further testimony by the prisoners of their treatment by the Marines. In other words, fuck the army, we're in charge. The supplement of C rations in their menu was withdrawn. Billy clubs maintained a constant rhythm on the doors of the cells, thwarting sleep. Those that complained were ordered to stand at attention pressed to the cell door while the Marines verbally abused them, while rapping on the mesh screen with their clubs, smarting the noses and chins of their wards. After two weeks of this treatment the disgruntled prisoners understood who was in charge. An understanding of sorts was reached; if there were no more complaints, there would be no more retaliation. There was no need to explain to those inhuman parasites, they knew the need for retribution. Most looked back on their own actions and felt they were not summarily given the true punishment they deserved. They had claimed death as punishment of transgressions by prisoners in their charge. Some of the prisoners smiled at the mildness of the treatment given them.

The fact that the witnesses could be left to roam the camp without constant surveillance disturbed Perlas and

Braxton. An incident occurred one quiet evening, clouds hung low, diffusing the illumination of a full moon. With no warning all the lights in the stockade and adjoining buildings went out. A cry of "Sergeant of the guard!" rang out. Perlas quickly entered the stockade. He was joined by Stoyon.

"We have to get the auxiliary generators going," said Perlas.

Drago asked, "You know how to start them?"

Perlas was quiet. Finally he said, "No, but Flint does, he's started these generators before. I have to find him."

There was a ruckus going on in one of the cells. The mad major was kicking the back of his Quonset hut. Strapped in the straitjacket, he devised a maneuver lying on his back with his feet kicking the plates in the rear of the hut, creating more noise than damage. Perlas ran to the cell, opened the door and whacked the major with his billy club. The blow would have killed anyone else; it just put the major out.

More Marines were running all over the stockade, some attempting to start the generators, others reinforced the complement guarding the cell blocks. All were unnerved.

Perlas appeared, dragging a groggy Cpl. Flint. Each generator had to be cranked to start. Flint went from generator to generator; they moaned and spit, and finally turned over. Flint engaged a switch; the motor produced the needed energy. The searchlights came on, only the towers were still darkened, they were not connected to the generators in the compound.

The Marines ordered all the prisoners to the cell doors. None of guards spoke Japanese, but the inflection in the voice of the guards demanded immediate compliance. All did as they were told except for the mad major.

"How did this happen?" Lt. Warren asked Perlas.

"Christ, I don't know, sir. It's a good thing Flint was around. Otherwise, we would have been screwed."

Cpl. Flint stood next to Perlas, one arm inert, the bone of his forearm had snapped. The crank, as all cranks were wont to do, snapped back before he could disengage his hand. It broke his arm. He was taken to the hospital. He remained there in a cast.

The searchlights attached to the generators were sending beams of light every which way. All of a sudden, the lights on the cell blocks came on. Braxton entered the stockade. He went up to Perlas. Drago joined them.

"They pulled the switch," Braxton said.

"What switch?" Perlas asked.

"The one controlling the current going into the stockade, one of them Japs we got roamin' around here must have pulled the switch," Braxton said angrily.

"Incredible. They sure made asses of us." Perlas intoned. "Now we have more of a problem here. How the hell are we going to protect ourselves from this bunch?"

A padlock was put on the switch box. The Japanese witnesses were rounded up, put on trucks and sent to a separate stockade. The only witnesses left at the criminal stockade were the ones needed to feed the internees, Cpl. Yamashita Tatsuo was among them. The Marines, if they knew, would have sent Tatsuo on his way, for he was the one fostering the minor insurrection.

Indecision

After the great blackout fiasco, guarding the prisoners became a chore for the Marines in Drago's outfit.

The war criminal stockade had one road coming into it. The whole camp was bordered by jungle on all four sides; to the north a stream sluiced a path to a tributary of the Pago River. A piece of cleared land to the south of the enclosure resembled a baseball diamond. Bats and balls were at a minimum, a few baseball gloves were available. A game of catch was initiated by two South Bronx aspiring big leaguers; otherwise the field was left unused.

Drago, walking from his quarters one evening to the mess hall, heard a rustling sound in the jungle off the road. His rifle hung over his shoulder. Since the extinguishing of the lights in the stockade, all Marines were ordered to carry their weapons wherever they went. He turned to the sound, took his rifle off his shoulder and placed a clip of ammunition into the chamber of the weapon.

He was torn. Should he sound an alarm or just fire into the foliage?

What if it's just an animal? You shoot it, and you'll look like a jack ass. It could be a renegade, or a witness, or maybe some marine out there takin' a piss. The situation angered him; he would rather have emptied the clip into the jungle.

"Come outta there! Ya better come outta there." There was no answer. He raised the rifle to his shoulder.

No answer. If it's a Jap, I'm dead, he thought. What was there lay still.

They're all around us, Drago conjectured, *and we're in the middle. This shit is unnerving. At least when you're in combat you have only one choice. You shoot, kill or be killed, that's the answer. Here, the choices you make could kill ya.*

Drago moved off. His decision to not fire into the jungle put him ill at ease. He walked further up the road. When a fair distance from the place where he heard the noise, he took two steps off the road into the jungle, where he waited. Whoever was there, he believed, would show themselves. After a time with no one's appearance, he gave up his vigil. Too many things about this duty left him in limbo. Garrison forces were strangled by military protocol: When instantaneous response was needed to save your ass from disaster you had to weigh your actions and that could put you in a casket.

I'm tired with this being indecisive. I'd rather be able to blast the bastards instead of holding back all the time. I know one thing: If I'm killed because of it no one is gonna give a shit.

He walked on, shouldering his rifle, perplexed.

Entertainment

The duty at the stockade became a trial of frayed nerves. There was an increase in bitching and a decrease in morale.

Perlas decided to do something about it. He went to the U.S.O. in Agana and arranged for a group of performers just arrived from the states to come to the camp and bring some entertainment to his men. They were rewarded by a promised evening of mirth and song.

A platform was raised in the center of the ball field. A plump singer past her prime arrived with a comic and a three piece band: a drummer, a saxophonist, and a trumpet player. The comic was raw; on the stage he mimicked both the first and second banana from a burlesque show. All laughed, the comic got a howl when he goosed the surprised plump singer. The show lasted about an hour.

The cooks spread out goodies: spam cut into small cubes, hardtack with cheese slices rounded out the fare.

After the show, the Marines mixed with the entertainers. That ended when one of the Marines, fortified with some green slimy looking booze, decided to see what was under the singer's skirt. The entertainers left.

The party was about to begin. Tom raided the sick bay and came away with a quart of alcohol, which he mixed with a gallon of fermented peaches provided by the mess sergeant. Five-gallon cans of peaches were set to fermenting under an enclosed bench. An eight-by-two board, five foot long, was placed over the mixture. The concoction exploded, sending fermented peaches as high as the highest point in the mess hall. A crew was sent out to clean up the mess.

A malt of sorts survived, which was then mixed with the sick bay alcohol, softening the concoction. The potency of the mixture was not diminished; Marines were lying all over the camp groaning. For awhile P.T. and Tom held their own, being the most fortified at all times. The night ended with Tom pummeling a guy by the name of Trodden, from Glen Cove, Long Island, he being the privileged son of the secondary school principal there, and the brother of a Marine Air Force pilot. Trodden was a snide son of a bitch. Sarcasm combined with a superiority complex, was bound to ignite someone's fuse, it happened to be Tom's. Tom stood under a tree, punching Trodden in the face, his head bouncing off the tree trunk with each blow. Since no one cared for Trodden, it was entertaining to see him pummeled. Drago watched the assault; Juarez came by and joined him. He tapped Drago on the shoulder.

"You think that's something," he pointed at the combatants. "Take a look up in the tree."

There, up about twenty feet, P.T. sat grinning with a canteen cup in his hand, the deadly mixture of peach punch overflowing. P.T. smiled down on them. His other hand wrapped around the tree. On seeing Drago and Juarez, he loosened his hold, made the sign of the cross and blessed them.

"How the hell did he get up there?" Drago questioned Juarez. "We don't have a ladder that can go that high."

The trunk of the tree could hold three men around it with arms out stretched and not touch one another.

"P.T., how'd you get up there?" Drago called up to the smiling Irishman.

P.T. just grinned, and took a sip of the brew.

"Okay P.T., how are you gonna get down?" Juarez asked.

P.T. sighed, but said nothing.

Tom finished his work on the boy from Glen Cove; he embraced both the corporals, and walked off with them.

"I'd say it's been one hell of a productive evening." Tom added, then burped.

The intoxicating liquor's emitted gasses forced the corporals to disengage themselves from the slobbering Tom. He was sent sprawling, confused as to why his comrades were angered.

The next morning, Drago and Perlas took a crew out to clean up the ball field. As they came nearer, the corporal was a bit confused. In the center of the diamond, a table and three chairs had been placed. Four bowls were on the table. He did not remember seeing them there the previous evening. He put the crew to picking up paper cups and other debris while he walked the area. P.T.'s tree was still there, but not the Irishman. He had not heard of any disaster, thus he assumed P.T. was all right. He went up to the table; small scraps of meat were left there along with some white rice, the rice was cooked, the bowls were empty.

We don't have rice eaters, except for the witnesses, and most are gone, except corporal Tatsuo and a dozen others to feed the prisoners. He would have to question Tatsuo about it.

~~~~~~~~~~~~~~

Drago classified the renegades as war criminals, the same as the prisoners in the War Criminal Stockade. When he finally caught up with them on another patrol, he would be judge, jury and executioner.

Remembering all that now at the hospital Stoyon was determined to again volunteer for any patrols that were hunting out the renegades. He could think of nothing else but to avenge the death of his friends. The grenades used to kill were American made; they must have been taken from the four Marines killed earlier. It was a definite move by the renegades to maim and to tell us, beware, we are still active.

Guilt plagued him. Should they have circumvented the perimeter of the Japanese encampment, instead of forming the skirmish line? He should have given more warning of what the possibilities of danger might be. The stay at the hospital occupied his time, not his mind.

The Disgruntled Swabby

Drago was tense, and wished at times he could not think, could just draw a blank: Those that could, he admired. The constant turmoil within tormented him. Release from the hospital became his goal; he intended to leave, if not with permission, then without.

His rage, though sublimated, exploded one evening. The ward he was in housed only Marines. They were there for a variety of ailments: bug bites, broken bones, torn muscles, and the testing of bodily fluids. The ward confined forty-two Marines in accommodations unheard of on the island: blankets, white bed sheets changed daily. The food was better than at base camp. Some of the Marines did not want to leave and worked out schemes to extend their stay.

Lights were out at nine or twenty-one bells. Bantering became the evening's entertainment. Jokes did not excuse the wards all-male attendants. Corpsmen were in abundance; raunchy reference to the sexual preferences of the attendants abounded.

The ward was checked each evening by sailors on guard duty. The corpsmen that had been assigned security duty carried pistols as required; they were also not immune to the scathing commentary of the Marines.

One evening, the guard on duty stopped before entering the ward and glared at the Marines. He snarled at the banter. Rather than participating and slandering the men in the ward, he fumed. The guard, bland, pale and thin of frame, wearing glasses, with his hand gripping the holstered pistol, entered the ward.

"You guys better shut up. Lights out; you're supposed to be quiet."

The Marines were stunned by his attitude. As he passed a bunk one of them said, "Fuck you!"

He turned around, trying to find the culprit.

"Who said that? You're on report. You guys think you own this place. We'll see about that."

Someone else laid out a raspberry through tongue and teeth. All laughed.

"Think you're smart, don't ya? You're all on report."

Drago wanted to thank the sailor; the incident diverted his mind from the turmoil there.

He addressed the guard. "Fer Christ sakes, lighten up, will ya?"

The corporal made a motion to get out of his bed and further address the disgruntled sailor. The guard withdrew his pistol from its holster, and raced to confront Drago. Fury had taken over.

"Get back in your bunk," he said, and pointed the pistol at the corporal.

"Whoa," Drago said. "Think of what you're doing!" He held out the flat of his hand to ward off the affront.

"I know what I'm doin'. I'm the guard here. Ya better do what I tell ya. You think you know everything." He waved the pistol under Drago's nose.

To a Marine, pointing a pistol at someone was intent to use it. It infuriated the Croat. He feigned submission, his eyes blazing.

Someone down the line of bunks said, "Piss off, you dope."

The sailor turned, and as he did Drago kicked him in the chest, then jumped off his bed and wrapped his arms around him. Two men on either side of Drago grabbed the agitated sailor; one tried to wrest the pistol from his hand, the other pinned his free arm to his back. Drago let loose his hold and smashed his fist into the man's face. The impact loosened two teeth from their moorings, and knocked him out. He dropped the pistol.

The young Croat addressed the group gathered around the dazed sailor.

"Let's tie this fucker up," Drago said, as he picked the pistol up off the deck.

Sheets were pulled off the bunks; they wrapped him as they would a mummy, and bound him with their belts. Drago grabbed the collar of the man's shirt.

"You guys stay here," he said to those gathered. "I'll take this shithead to the guard house."

He then towed the man out of the ward.

An orderly was sitting behind a desk in the hall, immobilized by the disturbance; in fear of the aggravated Marines, he tried to make himself as invisible as possible.

Drago confronted him. "Where's the officer of the day?"

"Down the hall, left at the end."

Drago dropped his charge, bent over the desk and thanked the invisible man. He picked up his package again with both hands. He reached the hall's end and turned left. At the far end of the extended hall sat a chief petty officer. A look of amazement crossed over his face as he noted the package being drawn to him.

"What the fuck's this all about?"

"Well, this asshole took his pistol out and threatened me with it," Drago removed the pistol from his pocket and put it on the petty officer's desk. "Put that big ass thing right under my nose."

"What the fuck for?" the officer of the day asked.

"Who knows? We were riding him; then he goes off the deep end. Stupid prick coulda killed one of us."

"Well, I'll be God-damned."

"Prick should be court-martialed. Ya don't point a gun at anyone unless you're gonna use it."

"Yeah, you're right. Listen, guy, I never would have thought this asshole would do a thing like that."

The bound sailor started to revive, was about to say something. The petty officer bent down, eyeballed him and said, "Shut the fuck up; you're in deep shit."

Then spoke to Drago, "Okay, I'll take it from here."

Drago was about to go, stopped, picked up the pistol, pointed it skyward released the clip, and laid both on the desk, then walked away.

He never found out what the outcome of the incident was, and didn't care. The petty officer's command of the situation put the corporal at ease. Peace reigned in the ward.

~~~~~~~~~~~~~

The underlying memory of the booby-trapped patrol still plagued him. His irritation at the forced inaction increased, to the point of demanding a quick release from the hospital. He developed a relationship of sorts with the attending physician. Doctor Johns had been on the beach at Iwo Jima and Okinawa; he admired the Marines for their fearless actions in combat. Drago would try to use the doctor's adulation to gain his release. If he could not, he had already decided to leave without permission.

Reflections

A full moon one evening drew him out of the ward; he found a place of peace, a covered clapboard walkway with wooden benches served as his sanctuary. He watched the tropical equatorial moon rise, a brilliant yellow orb encompassing three quarters of the horizon. Skeletal trees with war-torn branches created a patchwork on the face of the satellite, fascinating the young man. Nature; its beauty and fearsomeness enthralled.

I'll never see the likes of this again, he mused. *What an adventure this has been.*

His mind wandered.

Two typhoons last year, their power, sleeping men driven from Quonsets as roofs peeled. The wind blasted the corporal into the air; he flew, saved by a pole his arm embraced. Quonsets set on top of Quonsets.

A quake, its appearance not as frightening as would be expected, wonder prevailed. An exclamation of "Wow!" by P.T., and "Holy shit!" from Drago, as toiletries and various sundries left their moorings, while tent flaps and loosened tent pegs danced.

He remembered the transport leaving the states, the first night out. The transport blacked out, and he realized he was ascending into a new world that was fraught with danger. Sea and sky fomented into an unexpected prominence. The magic of the bow-sliced sea spraying florescent reminded him of sparklers on the 4th of July. The coal blackness of the night delivered a pockmarked flashing of stars.

Though he could not fathom the awakening of his senses, it cleansed his mind of the mundane. The adventure he was on was extraordinary. The pressing part was the life and death involved. His luck through it all amazed him. Then he remembered P.T., Jeremy and others gone, the thought of it pierced his heart. Never again were they to re-live the pleasures the earth fostered.

Another occurrence at the hospital crowned Drago's theory that life and death were controlled by the stupidity of others. The unraveling of that disturbing event happened in the same place that he stood now. One of the attendants was pushing a patient in a wheelchair. In it sat a black man, his body completely covered with four-by-four-inch squares. It left no doubt that his condition was dire.

Drago approached the attendant. "What's this about?" he questioned.

"Two Marines," the attendant stated. "Yeah, this guy and another one, ya see."

Drago was surprised; he had not seen any black Marines, certainly none in boot camp. He waited to hear more from the attendant.

"They're out there in the boonies, burnin' black powder. They're in supply, see, and some guy backs up a truck and dumps a load of powder on the pile already smoldering, and it blows up. Both are blown away and burned up bad. The other guy's already dead"

"Someone should have known better. Ya don't dump powder on a fire; it's like adding a fuse to it," Drago told the attendant.

Stoyon looked at the man in the wheelchair and could see the pain in his eyes. The attendant drew his hands from the wheelchair and motioned with his arms crossing in mime, intimating the patient was going to die. The attendant could sense the man's pain, as did the corporal.

"I just thought I'd get him out to see the sun shining. Christ, what can ya do for him?"

Drago tapped the attendant on the shoulder in attempt to let him know he understood his feelings. He walked away from them, and cursed under his breath.

Dumb shit, stupidity again, how many more times ya gonna hear about things like that? When will it be repeated? It freakin' never ends! The same old adage: Watch out for the guys who want to kill you, and stick with the ones are gonna help ya stay alive.

The Caucus

Obsession ruled; unjustified taking of life had to be revenged. He had to get back to the battalion. Doctor Johns was coerced into releasing Stoyon. Drago called the battalion for transportation; Perlas pulled up in a Jeep. They shook hands.

Two weeks passed. Drago became sullen. There had been no word coming forward regarding new patrols. The bulletin board contained the general work details, nothing more. Perlas and Braxton noticed the change in the corporal.

The sergeants remembered when the Croat had gone through another period of depression. The corporal came to them lamenting his condition.

"I gotta get outta here. I have to smell a woman. It's been a year now, ya can't go into any of the towns, everything is restricted. I don't know how you guys handle it."

But he did. There was a rumor of debauchery on a tugboat manned by the Seabees, captained by a chief petty officer whom Perlas had supplied with a freewheeling, foul-mouthed, blond, bosomy, Red Cross worker. The gift gave them access to an abundance of commissary goods unheard of on the island.

The Seabees in charge of unloading the ships in the harbor, although not involved in the labor, were the owners of all cargo. Cargo delegated to other branches of the service was not immune; if it was needed by Seabees, it belonged to them. This, of course, included booze. The tugs were floating castles, all tastes were satisfied: brandies, green Irish whisky, the finest Scotch, all became available to them. Perlas and Braxton used booze to ply the cooks in charge of the officer's mess out of steaks. The C.P.O. on the tug was glad to cooperate with the sergeants. Of course, access to these delicacies also induced some of the local villagers to free their offspring in exchange for available commissary. It was said the lack of comeliness of the indentured females was offset by zeal.

An arrangement involving Lieutenant Warren, Perlas, and Braxton was a stroke of genius. Warren was going to a dinner dance at Naval Staff Headquarters. The dance was a private gathering by invitation only; he was the only Marine officer asked from the battalion.

His reputation as a nut job was veiled, so the recipients of his company felt they were in the presence of a real live hero. His combat prowess gave him status that opened doors for the first lieutenant. All those attending the dance were of staff and associated personnel on the island.

All the available femininity, of either aboveboard or devious character, were to be present.

"If the kid can't make out there, there's gotta be something wrong," said Warren.

The three formed a caucus. Warren proposed a deception, which if exposed, would send them all before the adjutant general. When Warren suggested it, they could not believe it. He, Warren, would get an officers' uniform that fit the corporal; Drago would dress in the uniform, including the bars of a second lieutenant; over it he would put his fatigues. They would ride out of the post together. Drago was to strip off the fatigues, and partners in the deception, they would enter the banquet.

"Listen, kid, this is not only about you," Warren explained, "I got this great lookin' gal I've been tryin' to get alone since Christ knows when. She's got this sister, see. I want you to occupy her while I'm makin' a move on the other one."

The conspirators entered the banquet hall. They met their quarry. Drago had seen a lot since entering the Corps. There were times when fear governed; the first day in boot camp took precedence, and again before his initiation into combat; during it all he controlled his bowels. The night of the banquet, he thought he was going to pee in his pants.

Lieutenant Warren pointed out Sarah, Drago's partner for the evening. Sarah relinquished the surveillance of her sister and went off to dance with Drago. She noticed the fear in the bogus lieutenant's face, and, offering him her hand, they left their companions for the dance floor. Her red hair moved about her head, flashing and gilding into fascinating shades of burgundy. They danced. She whirled on the dance floor in green print calico, effervescent and confident. She laughed with Drago. Her perfumed body touched off a blaze in the impostor. He, trying to control the fire, maintained space between them. She, the spoiler, drew him to her, smiling as she did.

Shit, Drago thought. *Let it go.*

The blaze ignited. He became hard; she pressed closer.

The huge Quonset where the affair was held abutted the beach. The two left the dance floor and walked along the sand. The beach was lined with palm trees. She was leading Drago. He reluctant, she insisting, she guided him to a palm tree set back behind the others facing the beach. Putting her back to the tree, she drew him to her. Her breasts floated under his massage; her pelvis probed his groin. Submission pervaded. Warm lips pursed and engaged softly in contrast to the aggressiveness of their engaged organs. They consummated their thirst pinned to the palm tree.

Walking back to the dance hall hand in hand, she rested her head on his chest, alternately brushing his cheek with lips and the palm of her hand. They stopped before entering the quasi-banquet hall. She whispered into his ear.

"You are a contradiction, sir. I know who you are. You're a prince, an impostor, a genesis of the plains; you are Corporal Stoyon. My handsome prince; I adore you."

"Warren told you beforehand, didn't he? Oh Jesus Christ!"

She smiled at Drago. He smiled back at her.

Lieutenant Warren was waiting for them. He winked at the girl, she walked past the lieutenant and as she did, she affectionately touched his arm.

"Let's get out of this joint," he said to the corporal. Reluctantly, Drago said goodbye to Sarah.

Before driving back to the base, they cut off the road, where Drago was handed his fatigues. He changed, leaving the impostor in the back of the Jeep.

Drago thought, *Goodbye and good luck. I'll never see her again, but I'll remember, I'll remember.*

As they entered the base, he looked at the lieutenant and said, "Thanks, sir."

The lieutenant playfully pinched the corporal on the arm.

"Shit, boy, we fooled 'em. Ain't that a kick in the ass?" The lieutenant offered a wide grin to the impostor.

"Yeah we fooled 'em," returned Drago, "thanks."

Drago's Decision

Drago had not approached the sergeants about his concerns since coming back from the hospital, but the melancholia he carried about did not go unnoticed. One day Perlas approached him.

"What's goin' on, kid?"

"I'll ask you the same question. I don't see any action on any patrols; I thought we'd get some notice by now."

"Well, kid, we're not involved any more. It seems the Air Force is taking over. We've been informed they are going into the interior with bull horns, and they are going to try to get the Japs out of there."

Drago became agitated. "What happened there is our business; it's Marine business. We got six dead out there fer nothin'. Ya think the Air Force gives a shit about that? Those so-called renegades killed our friends; we have to go back there."

He made a fist trying to control his anger.

"Don't get involved, Drago. It ain't gonna be worth it. You do anything crazy and it'll cost ya."

"I know the cost, Sarg. I know the rules, you know that. I ain't gonna let it sit like that. It's not their problem, it's the Corps. They're gonna let 'em walk out of there bowing and chanting their gibberish all the way back to Japan. Ya know why: 'cause they got their last licks in. They killed P.T. and McVey; they were my friends. I can't let it be that way."

Perlas had been associated with the corporal for fifteen months now, and never before had seen him so irritated.

"Listen, Drago, you got that third stripe comin', you're doin' good, let it alone."

"There's just things ya can't let pass, Sarg." He walked away from Perlas.

The next day he sought out Juarez. "I gotta talk to you about something, it's important."

"Okay, I got nothin' to do, let's do it."

"I'm goin' back in," Drago said.

"In where?" questioned Juarez.

'I'm goin' back in the jungle after them fuckers that killed P.T. and McVey."

"You can't do that! Are you crazy?"

"I'm fuckin' tired of people calling me crazy. All I want is some help in getting some gear together. Those guys in charge of supply are Puerto Ricans from the Bronx. Take 'em under your wing for about an hour while I get the stuff I need."

"What the hell's come over you? You don't know how many of them are in that jungle. Wait, maybe we'll get another patrol started soon." Juarez tried to forestall him.

"Not a chance. The fly boys got in; we're out."

"No, first we'll go to the colonel and tell him how you feel."

"I already talked to Perlas; he says we're out of luck. It's not our business anymore."

"I'll go to the colonel with you. If it gets you nowhere, I'll help you."

The next morning, they were received by the new commander, a silver-leaf light colonel, and the first sergeant. They pleaded their case, retold the story of the patrol and stressed the need for the Marines to do the job of accosting the renegades. The new commander, Lieutenant Colonel Kramer, asked the first sergeant for the communiqué from island command regarding their position. The sergeant, always on the ready, handed it to him. The colonel looked sad, but quoted directly from the sheet, then said, "It's not our business anymore. You are dismissed."

After leaving the office, Juarez said to Drago, "Tomorrow afternoon I'll get a Jeep. First, we'll get you what you need from the quartermasters. I'll take care of the Ricans." Juarez held his hand out to Drago; he took it in gratitude.

The next day, Juarez plied the two Puerto Ricans away from the quartermaster's stores with an offer of a pack of cigarettes for their knowledge of some fair maiden that he could correspond with in the States.

Drago entered the storeroom and proceeded to fill his needs: A dozen K rations, an extra canteen, four clips of ammunition, two grenades, and an extra first aid kit. He left the quartermasters pleased with his acquisitions.

Juarez, driving a Jeep, picked him up that evening. They proceeded to their destination across from Talofofo Bay where they had entered the jungle on the last patrol. They sat in the Jeep as the sun was setting by the bay. The mast of a Japanese freighter protruding from the surf where the ship sank created an elongated V reaching to the horizon.

"Ya know, I'm scared, but I gotta do this," Drago admitted.

"Maybe you want to change your mind," said Juarez.

"Nah, I guess it's the Hungarian in me. We're all kinda thick-skulled. Listen, Juarez, if I don't get out of this, explain it to Perlas and Braxton. My ass is gonna be in a sling anyway."

"What about your family?"

"No, it's not like they give a shit. Let that be."

"Keep your head about ya; you know how dangerous they are."

Drago was surprised that Juarez did not try harder to talk him out of his expedition. He should not have been. Corporal Juarez was a person who understood the importance of a mindset; his own values demanded he not pursue it further. Drago left the Jeep and entered the jungle as the sun was setting.

Going Home

P.T.'s body was met by his brothers at the train station in Chicago. Shawn was destroyed by the loss. He constantly covered his face with his hands, sobbing uncontrollably. He and Patrick accompanied the body to the waiting hearse. Mother O'Rielly waited in their flat, a handkerchief balled in the palm of her hand. She tried to act the part of the bereaved under control, but the tears welled and overflowed. From the depths rose the thought of Peter Thomas and the pixies: her lovely boy destroyed. When first told of his death, she did not believe the sergeant bringing her the message.

"Oh, the war is over; my boy isn't dead! How could that happen to my boy? Why would they want to kill my boy? Who are the people that wanted to kill my Peter Thomas?"

Mrs. O'Rielly looked to her daughter Mary for consolation. Mary was crying; she took her mother's hand. An easing of their pain came about as they held one another. As they waited for the boys to come back from the funeral home, both tried not to picture the affable broad smile of Peter Thomas, for fear of breaking down entirely.

~~~~~~~~~~~~~~

Jeremy McVey's father drove his truck to the train station; he would pick up his son's body there. He brushed sand with a twig to pass the time. The coffin was put in the well of the truck. Jeremy's father was solemn on the return trip to the farm. As with the O'Reillys, he could not understand why his son was killed. The sergeant attending the body told him they went into the jungle to root out renegade Japanese that had killed four Marines. Jeremy, he felt, went on the patrol to avenge the death of those Marines. As with most Americans, the thought of death to foster a noble cause was acceptable. If the truth were told, it would not have set well with Jeremy's father. It happened to be a case of boredom, the need for an adventure. A nagging need to test one's self, and wondering how he would fare in combat, made him volunteer. Jeremy often thought of the bombardment by the enemy of the beachheads the Marines invaded: Could he stand up to it? The patrol was his answer; he would be tested there.

Jeremy, like Stoyon, was a regular Marine. Jeremy enlisted in 1945 for the mandatory four years. Had he waited for a testing, the Korean War would have started. Jeremy McVey joined the ranks of all men on the border of war; those not participating in combat for whatever reason live with a nagging uncertainty of what their actions would have been if they had participated. Jeremy's test was over.

The coffin bounced around in the back of the truck.

Death was not new to Jeremy's sisters. Farms brought death to animals for food; chicken, cows, pigs, all were needed for sustenance. His father expounded to the children Jeremy's heroics in volunteering for the patrol. The girls alternately went to the hay loft where they had frolicked with their brother, and sobbed their hearts out.

Mother McVey collapsed in her husband's arms when she heard the news from the sergeant delivering the message. She was put to bed. Her husband joined her after tucking the girls in. Putting his arms around her to comfort her, he felt her pain. The finality of the death of her son overwhelmed her; she sobbed throughout the night.

At dawn, her bereavement subsided as her role became clear: she was to give comfort to her family and those who would participate in the ceremony for the deceased. Father McVey contacted the Marines for a military funeral. Jeremy would be interred in the military cemetery overlooking the stone quarry. He remembered how the boy enjoyed swimming there.

Book 2

The Renegades

The Shooter—October 1945

Siko Hiroshi watched from the fringe of the jungle as two of his comrades, Itaro and Keiji, approached the patrol of Marines just south of the Talofofo river bed. The Marines had their weapons pointed at the Japanese soldiers. Itaro had a rolled up leaflet tucked under his arm; as he reached for it, one of the Marines shot him. He fell forward. The other Japanese soldier was stunned; he stood there awaiting his fate. All rifles were turned on him. He raised his hands above his head, letting the Marines know he had no weapon.

The shooter approached the fallen man. He looked down at him aghast at finding not a weapon as he thought, but a leaflet dropped from B-25 bombers into the jungle. The message told of the capitulation of hostilities as decreed by the Emperor of Japan. There was no remorse in the killing of the Japanese soldier by the shooter. He remembered how throughout all the campaigns his comrades were deceived and annihilated by their treachery. The Marine cursed the dead man.

"What the hell he reach for that thing for? I thought he had a God damn gun! Jesus, H. Christ. Shit, ya never know what these pricks are gonna do. He could have had a gun! Ya know? Oh, shit!" He addressed his comments to the rest of the patrol.

A second Marine reprimanded the shooter. "We're supposed to take these fuckers in, fer Christ sakes. Ya got trigger happy. What the hell we gonna do now?"

The shooter defended his action. "Shit, ya know how they are; he coulda had a gun, ya know, and killed all of us."

The Japanese soldier with his hands up, began to tremble; the exchange from the Marines made him panic. He looked for an escape; there was none. All weapons were poised and ready. "What the hell we gonna do with this one? He sure as hell is gonna open his mouth about what happened." The shooter looked at the dead man, and then at the one with the raised arms, and shot him. "That's the end of that shit. Let's get the hell outta here. We don't have to worry about it any longer."

No one spoke; they proceeded on their way. The shooter placed his rifle over his shoulder, his hand on the trigger guard. *There's a lot more Japanese in the jungle here, and a lot more to worry about,* he rationalized.

Siko Hiroshi was enraged at the killing. He silently fumed. The patrol advanced in his direction. Hiroshi ran, the growth about him slashing at his body; he took no care to deceive. The noise of his retreat alerted the Marines; through habit they sprayed the area with their ordinance. Hiroshi tripped; as he lay there bullets passed over him. After the first burst, they stopped firing.

"See, what did I tell ya, them sons a bitches are all over this fuckin' jungle," said the shooter.

The shooter's action was justified, in the eyes of his mates. The patrol felt less guilty about the incident.

Yeah, I've seen guys blown away by these cock-knockers, the shooter fumed inwardly. *What does one more or less of them mean? They outta all fuckin' die. Even killing them could get your ass hung. The reason we're here is 'cause three dumb ass Marines got blasted while out lookin' for souvenirs. They'll never stop shootin' back at us. Give up, bullshit. We've killed two of them; there's more of 'em out here want to put us in a grave.*

Cpl. Hiroshi ran for ten minutes. He finally found an area where the growth was thick; he knew from other patrols they would not follow him there. He sat, his mind returning to before the shooting. Hiroshi was learned; he could read, both of his companions could not. He read the contents of the leaflet to them, and pointed out the errors in grammar.

"The Emperor would not say that. If it was from him it would be more eloquent. This paper is a lie. I tell you, we must hold out and do as much damage to the Americans as we possibly can, and wait for our comrades' return. Stay with us. With the cache of arms we have we can trouble them."

The Americans would pay for their treachery. Hiroshi would avenge his brothers in arms.

The Alliance

The men in Hiroshi's cadre included Sergeant Superior Nakamura Toshio, Privates Akira Isamu, and Itaro and Keiji. The six of them had gathered together in close proximity. Itaro and Kiji had not heeded Hiroshi's warning about the treachery of the Americans; they were now dead.

It would have been better to commit Seppuku rather than be shot while disgracing your body and soul by surrendering. There is no room in the ever-after, the glorious ascension, for those who would cower before the enemy. Their bodies will forever be unclean; their souls stagnant on the earth. Hiroshi damned his comrades, then sat and prayed for them.

Later that evening, he went back to the area of the encounter, found them and buried them. The incident had to be reported to Sgt. Nakamura. The sergeant's place of hiding was so secure it was difficult to find him. Nakamura usually went to the river bed for water in the evening; Hiroshi waited for him there.

Nakamura moved with stealth to the river. Caution prevailed since they killed the two Marines. He was angry that one of them had escaped; otherwise the bodies would not have been discovered. The American patrols were more constant; he only moved at night. He wished to fill the two American canteens he carried. The stream was very clean, and had a steady flow. From the survival training he received in Manchukuo, he knew that moving water was the safest water to drink. As he filled the canteen, he heard a noise; he turned, expecting death. Hiroshi whispered his name.

"Sergeant Nakamura, it is I, Hiroshi. Do not be alarmed."

Nakamura made a mental note never to leave his quarters again without his rifle, yet he was glad he did not have it; otherwise he would have shot Hiroshi.

"Why do you come to me in this manner? I have told you if I needed you or the others I would find you. It is not good to search me out; it gives the Americans knowledge of our positions."

Hiroshi realized before they were living as animals in the jungle Nakamura Toshio would surely have given him a beating for his indiscretion. It had changed now that they depended on each other for their survival.

"Where are the rest of your companions?"

"Two are dead. Itaro and Keiji, killed by the Americans.

He did not wish to explain their attempted surrender; it was enough that they were disgraced in his eyes alone.

"How did it happen?"

He told Nakamura a tale of an ambush by the river.

"I told you not to travel by day. Do you think my wishes are to be disregarded?" Hiroshi did not answer.

Nakamura sent Hiroshi away. Hiroshi went back to the cave by the river where he, Itaro and Keiji lived. He was now alone. Later, he would find Akira and Isamu requesting they join him there. The cave opening was high above the ground. There were a number of handholds which had to be negotiated to ascend. During the day, it was easy to climb; at night it became precarious. Slowly and cautiously he searched for the handholds. Finally succeeding, he crawled into the slit in the earth that was home.

His only solace in living in the bowl of earth was the valued rifles and ammunition they had foraged after the Americans left the battlefield. There were two M1 rifles with ample ammunition. A Japanese Nambu machinegun still ensconced in cosmoline. With no ammunition, it was useless. Two American hand grenades and a Japanese light mortar with two shells completed the arsenal.

He lay there remembering all that happened since the final battle, when the Marines laid down a horrific artillery barrage. His Major Goto was felled by an exploding shell. An American officer, recognizing the insignia on the major's tunic, and knowing the value of capturing an officer of rank, instructed his men to bind him. The major, upon awakening, could do nothing but froth at the mouth and curse his captors. He was summarily silenced by a well-placed rifle butt. It became a mission for the major to cause as much distress as possible to the Marines.

At first, they bound his hands; Goto tried running away. Still in a daze from the concussion, he did not get very far; a passing sergeant laid a right cross to his jaw; he went down. The sergeant instructed the men to bind his feet also.

Hiroshi played dead on the battlefield. Lying there, he watched as the Americans gathered those that could no longer resist. He was not discovered. That evening, the enemy withdrew. Hiroshi dashed into the jungle; there he met Atiro and Keiji. Later they came across Nakamura, Akira and Isamu.

A year after the Americans secured the island, Hiroshi and the others could move about the jungle during the day without fear of being observed. At night, they moved around wherever they pleased.

Their primary objective became the acquisition of food. Nakamura instructed them in the art of setting traps to catch shrimp and eels in the estuaries of the Talofofo River. His knowledge of plants that were edible and their foraging helped them supplement their meager diet. Still, they were always near starvation.

The Marines of the 9th Antiaircraft Battalion, while on the hill in a tent camp just above the Talofofo inlet, unknowingly supplied them with food. Nakamura's band would wait for evening to raid the dumpster behind the American officers' mess. The mess hall was in line with a walking post. They waited in the foliage for the guard to pass, and then they would scour the dumpster and the grounds around it for whatever scraps were available. At times they would acquire discarded bags of potatoes or cans of meat half-devoured. Mostly, they fed on the scraps the officers left.

It would be easy to kill the man on the post as he passed the mess hall; the vegetation canopied the roof there. They did not harm the posted guards for fear of losing their alternate supply of food.

The Marines abandoned the tent camp for better quarters in the Agana district. With the loss of the dumpster supply, Hiroshi and his companions became more daring in their hunt for food. They donned the khaki uniforms of the souvenir hunters they had murdered, then left their sanctuary at dusk and brazenly traversed the roads at night. A vehicle would pass them on the road and they would wave to the occupants; if the Jeep or truck stopped, they would disappear into the foliage on either side of the road. On looking back, the drivers seeing no one there, shrugged and went about their business.

Once, a passing Jeep abruptly turned around, drove back and stopped where they were seen entering the jungle. The single passenger in the Jeep wasted no time in spraying the area with his weapons. Sgt. Killian always carried a Browning automatic rifle, a carbine, and a .45 pistol when he went out. After firing all the ammunition he had available, he shouted as he scanned the jungle.

"Motherless whores, cock-sucking fuckin' Jap bastards. Show your fuckin' faces, you whore eatin' pricks! I'll cut your balls off and feed 'em to the cows, you motherless shit-heads. You shit-eatin' sons a bitches better watch out for me. I'll come back and stick a bayonet up your asses. I can smell ya; my nose will tell me where you are, and I'll cut ya up and feed the parts to the fuckin' snakes. You'll never see your ancestors when I get through with ya. You're all a bunch of whores anyway."

Hiroshi, Akira and Isamu were buried in the turf while the fusillade passed over them; they listened to the tongue-lashing the gunnery sergeant spat out at them. They did not move. The sergeant spewed more abuse as he entered his Jeep, then sped off.

Hiroshi felt a kinship with the orator; his lack of fear reminded him of many other American soldiers who came upon them in battle. They were willing to face certain death to save another's life. It was stupid, he thought, but amazingly brave. He also remembered that with them there was little waste of life, if it could be avoided. They never initiated a foolish attack. He saw many of his own people destroyed in banzai attacks; he participated in two, but came out unscathed.

Friends & Enemies

They went out regularly and stayed off the road during the day watching the Americans. They were hardly disturbed, and became more brazen.

On one occasion, they came across a stockade in a cleared out area of the jungle. They sat off the road that circumvented the enclosure. To their front, an overhang of sheet metal had many cots underneath lined up in rows. About twenty Japanese soldiers were standing in line waiting; another was busy dolling out portions of rice to them. Hiroshi recognized the man dispensing the food as one from his company. They waited until he finished serving, and as he carried the huge pot up the road, now nearly empty, Hiroshi called to him.

"PSST, PSST! Tatsuo, it's Hiroshi."

Tatsuo was so startled; he dropped the pot, then quickly looked around towards the stockade. He turned again to the foliage and saw no one.

"Come here Tatsuo, it is Hiroshi."

Hiroshi stood up and beckoned Tatsuo to come to him. Tatsuo, finally spotting him, reclaimed the pot and dashed into the jungle.

"Hiroshi, Hiroshi, I thought you dead! What are you doing hiding here? The war is over, we have lost, you should not hide any longer. Go and give yourself up. There is another encampment with thousands of us on the island. They feed us, and say we will be sent home. We are disgraced, but alive, and have heard a radio program where the Emperor told us to cooperate with the Americans," he rapidly exclaimed.

"What is this enclosure?" asked Hiroshi. "And why are you as free as a bird?"

"They have here what they call 'war criminals.' Major Goto is here, he is distraught, he wished to commit Seppuku, but was thwarted by the Americans. His crime, it is said, was that he killed American soldiers after they surrendered. I remember they fought so valiantly; still, they enraged the major when they laid down their arms. He took his sword and decapitated them. Is that wrong? It is a disgrace to be captured. They will try him, and hang him.

"I am to be what they call a witness; I must testify against the major. This is the edict set down by the Emperor. Why do you not surrender? They treat us well."

Hiroshi told Tatsuo about the two men who tried to surrender, then were killed by the Marines, and about the leaflet being a fake. Tatsuo was puzzled.

"It is possible we were wrong to surrender; we shall be degraded throughout eternity. God help us." Tatsuo brought his hands up in prayer. He continued.

"My major is bound hand and foot. He tried to escape. He kicked out the metal panel from the back of his cell. The soldiers waited for him and as he emerged they bludgeoned him severely. They have prevailed upon me to attend the major when he takes his meals. I was not to talk to him while I fed him. Goto made a terrible row. I spoke to him; my conversing with the major calmed him, it pleased the guards. I am allowed to converse with him further. The major and I made plans for his escape. I turned off the generators that illuminated the enclosure by disengaging the switch. The Americans are foolish. There was no one guarding the generators; it was a simple task.

"The lights were extinguished. The major then tried to kick out the back panel of the cell again, but it was reinforced with chains because of his last attempt. In the end, his action was thwarted by a burly sergeant, one of the most in control in the administration of the compound. He must be dealt with cautiously."

"Quiet, I hear someone coming!" said Hiroshi.

The words uttered startled Akira, he fell over backwards noisily; it alerted a passing Marine. It was Cpl. Drago Stoyon. On hearing the disturbance, Drago removed his rifle from his shoulder, and pointed it in the direction of the noise. He called out to them to come out. He surveyed his entire front. The renegades expected to be shot at. They should not have feared. Any firing would alert the entire camp; he would be reprimanded for unnecessarily sounding the alarm. Drago held back from firing. Reluctantly, he moved off a distance, and entered the jungle. He stood there for fifteen minutes, and with no sound coming from the undergrowth, he decided whatever danger there was had passed. He moved on.

Tatsuo was the first to speak after the corporal left.

"It is good he did not alert the rest of the soldiers, but you must be very careful of that one; he is very smart. One day on inspection of the cells, I was there to interpret. My English I learned in the United States, it is very bad. Sometimes I do not tell them exactly what is said by the prisoners. They would surely beat them if they knew how they demeaned their captors.

"A colonel taken from the island of Chi Chi Jima was eyeing the pistol of this stupid American lieutenant; it was within reach and could easily have been taken from its holster. The colonel looked at the others in the inspection party, and saw the corporal watching him. He smiled at the corporal. The corporal brought his club up and smiled back as he pressed the baton into the colonel's belly. The colonel stepped back and knew that his idea of escaping was gone. I watched it all."

"So what are you about?" asked Tatsuo after finishing his story.

Hiroshi answered, "We have seen enormous supplies when we came down from the hills. It is time for us to destroy them. We are committed; there can be no other way for us. I am going to talk to sergeant Nakamura to see if he will help us."

"Ah, Nakamura is one of you." Tatsuo seemed surprised that the sergeant survived.

"We have ambushed many Americans and have enough ammunition to accomplish our mission. We shall be diligent and purposeful to the end." Hiroshi gave notice of their intent.

"I will not deter you from your aims, nor will I alert the Americans of your plans. So be it for now," promised Tatsuo.

Tatsuo placed his palms together, and bowed his head, blessing the activist.

"The Americans are going to have entertainment this evening. When they partake they become very foolish, I have seen it in their country. It is possible we can take advantage of the situation. There is an open field on the far side of the camp; the Americans play baseball there, it has no light. After dark no one goes there. I will go to the field kitchen and fill this container with rice and some meat. I shall leave it for you. You must remain quiet and hidden until all is clear. Then I will come for you."

Tatsuo left them. At the mess tent, no one questioned his taking extra food. He hid the pot. The Americans reveled in their drunkenness, then at dusk, retired. Later, Tatsuo placed a table and chairs he acquired on the pitcher's mound of the baseball diamond. A full moon illuminated the banquet. They ate and were not disturbed. The men stationed on the towers did not turn their heads towards the ball field.

Hiroshi

Hiroshi sat by his father's side and waited for him to finish a pair of sandals. When completed, he would take them to the patron for whom they were made. There were times when he had to go great distances to deliver his father's wares. Hiroshi ran and let his mind play, imagining a throng at a track meet shouting his name. He would be the Olympic hopeful the Japanese people would be cheering, Hiroshi running a marathon. By his side others of lesser nations would keep pace; then he would sprint wildly, outdistancing the nearest competitor.

When delivering his father's wares, he would walk through the town or village streets as the victor, beaming. Those on seeing him enter often wondered who this person was coming into their midst with a defiant stride and mocking smile on his lips. The patron receiving would notice that Hiroshi's demeanor was less than submissive as would be expected of a delivery boy. Word spread, and his attitude could no longer be tolerated by his father's patrons. As an affront, they would send a servant to deal with his arrogance. Many would not commission his father again. The cobbler could not understand the reason for his decline in business; not knowing made Hiroshi's father suspect his workmanship was lacking, and not up to the standards expected.

Hiroshi's boldness was seen by a comely servant of one of his father's patrons as a confidence and assurance hardly seen by those in their circle. She made a point of being on hand whenever Hiroshi would be about. His stature alone made him stand out. At six feet he stood at least a head taller than the men in the surrounding villages. His stance reminded the servant girl of a straight stave of bamboo, strong and stable. His shoulders were broad and his shaven head gave the appearance of one whose ancestors were of noble birth.

The servant became enamored with Hiroshi. They would meet, and she would bring prepared delicacies for him. Hiroshi accepted, and also found a willing recipient of his aspirations. He explained his dreams and the means by which he expected to accomplish them to her. It meant little to the servant girl; she could not see beyond her being one with him.

The liaison ended when Hiroshi realized that Semi the servant girl adored him. His arrogance exploded when, in seclusion, her subtle snuggling was rewarded by a bestial attack. He tore her clothes off, and threw her forcibly to the floor. She misconstrued his ardor as a lust for her alone. She gave in to him. Once inside her, his ferocity became uncontrollable. He tore her, and when she whimpered he stifled her cries by pressing his hand over her mouth, and continued to probe her grotesquely. She cried, and realized the perceived ardor of this man she had chosen was rape.

Consummation was not to be his; he continued to rip her. Sumi's body finally gave notice to her, and to relieve her pain and sorrow, she fainted. Hiroshi worked on the inert body for half an hour; still he could not ejaculate. His efforts ended in anger and frustration. His blame for failure lay solely with raped woman. In his mind's view she was unworthy. Hiroshi always negated any doubts cast on his manhood by transference of blame. He snorted at the crushed body as he left her.

Hiroshi found soldiering useful for quelling his pent-up energy, as well as his frustrations.

The Hermit

Hiroshi waited at the stream with Akira and Isamu for Sergeant Nakamura. A signal was instituted: Hiroshi would whistle a single note to alert the sergeant that they were in the vicinity. If he heard it, he would appear. Nakamura, silent and ghostly, stood at a distance, listened, and watched the three. He spoke from his position.

"You men are such fools! If I were the Americans, you would be dead. I have been standing here many minutes and listened to your chatter. What is it you wish of me?"

Nakamura was annoyed. He was settled into his hermetic existence, happy to be alone. It was as he lived in Japan: he gathered herbs, tubers, and mushrooms in the remote mountainous area in the North Country. He would be gone for weeks at a time. For sustenance, he carried with him five pounds of rice, and gathered succulent roots and tubers, these he cooked over an open fire. The sale of his gatherings, though not lucrative, had provided him with a modest income. He only looked to survive.

Nakamura's dugout in the jungle was quite comfortable. There were many fibrous plants in the area; some could be woven into cloth, from which he would make clothing. Trapping shrimp and eels added protein to his diet. He needed no one. He wished to leave his soldiering in the past.

"We have come to tell you we have found huge enemy supplies in the north. We wish you to join us in their destruction. Destroying them will cause them much pain. We have the light mortar and two mortar shells; we will take them with us. There are not many guards; it should not be hard to do," said Hiroshi.

"If you do this, you will alert the Americans, and they will come for us. I will not come with you, but will give you my blessing in your endeavor," replied Nakamura.

Hiroshi silently fumed. Every time he came up with a plan, it was discounted by the sergeant as a threat to their existence. Still, he was the superior, and his sergeant, whatever his wishes, they must be obeyed. They parted.

The Supply Depot

The next day, the leftover rice from Tatsuo was placed in a cloth sack, and with the mortar and the two shells, Hiroshi's band of renegades prepared to leave without their sergeant. It would take them a full day to get to the supply depot. The knowledge of the danger involved did not deter them; they were prepared. The mission had to be carried out in the daytime. With the mortar they had to account for the trajectory, needing to see their objective; also working the lanyard mechanism required an open space. Their scouting was complete; a depression just on the edge of the jungle hid them from view.

~~~~~~~~~~~~~~~

The Seabee petty officer, second class, backed the flatbed truck on the far side of the ammunition dump. He could not be seen from the main gate of the supply depot, where the ordnance was piled high. He turned off the ignition, brought his feet up on the seat and rested his head on the open window.

~~~~~~~~~~~~~~~

Hiroshi and his companions, Akira and Isamu, placed the concave base of the mortar in the sand surrounding the supplies. Akira slowly loaded the shell into the tube. Isamu held the cylinder's arc so that it would send the shell to the center of the cache. Hiroshi held the lanyard, on Akira's signal he pulled. Isamu's hold on the tube loosened from the force Hiroshi put on the lanyard.

~~~~~~~~~~~~~~~

The American petty officer flinched as the mortar careened off the gasoline drums behind him. *What's that, somebody workin' around here? I'd better get out of here*, he said to himself. He started the motor and, assuming it in a forward gear, he accelerated. The truck, in reverse, backed into some oil drums at the same time the second mortar shell exploded. The force of the explosion rocked the entire island.

Drago, out with a group policing their camp, felt the ground tremble, then watched as a plume of smoke rose into the air.

The petty officer was hurled into the air, his body torn apart. All that remained were torn bits of denim scattered a hundred yards from the center of the explosion. Later, a member of the cleanup crew slipped a patch with two red stripes guarded by a silver eagle into his pocket. The petty officer was tried in absentia for backing his truck into the gasoline drums and causing the catastrophe.

The renegades had not expected the blast would be so great. The force of it threw them into the air. Isamu was ecstatic, his body flying, the weightlessness made him smile. His body struck a tree; death was so instantaneous it could not erase his smile. Hiroshi and Akira were thrown into a mud-hole two feet from Isamu. The concussion stunned them; they lay there in a daze.

The shock of the blast wore off just as the area erupted into a hive of activity. Trucks of all description unloaded personnel and equipment trying to contain the blaze caused by the explosion. Though stunned, the Japanese crawled into the jungle only a few feet away from the work party, dragging Isamu's body with them.

Evening came. The work party quenched the blaze as best they could, and then departed. The renegades emerged from the jungle to see what damage they had done. To their surprise, all around them were packages marked with a circle and a large K in the center. Hiroshi opened one, and discovered their new found supply of food: a bonus, God-given, to thank them for their efforts in destroying the American supply depot.

They buried their comrade in the jungle. Hiroshi made a mental note of where they interred him.

When we retake this island I will find the dead and give them all a proper burial, he silently vowed.

They removed their clothes, made sacks out of them and stuffed them with their supply of K-rations. Hiroshi and Akira opened one of them and gleefully ate the small chocolate bar it held.

~~~~~~~~~~~~~~

Nakamura felt the shock wave of the explosion, as did all the residents of the island. He assumed Hiroshi had accomplished his mission. It pleased him; he wondered if he would see them again.

To his surprise, Hiroshi arrived and distributed some of the rations to him. Having not participated in their raid, he was ashamed to accept them. Nakamura Toshio bowed his head in thanks to Hiroshi. His position as superior was now diminished with the acceptance. His pride damaged, he had to reclaim face. He would find a way.

P.O.W. Stockade and the Buddha

Tatsuo was summoned to the office of the commander of the war Criminal stockade. Tatsuo feared he had been discovered initiating the blackout and feeding Hiroshi's group. His fears were unfounded. Lt. Warren, in charge, sat at a desk, with Sgt. Perlas by his side.

"Tatsuo," Perlas growled. "We are going to send you and Corporal Stoyon to the stockade in Agana. You are to pick up a prisoner by the name of Matsuki Ioto; he will be brought here to join the rest of the witnesses. You can wait outside for the corporal."

Tatsuo bowed and left the tent. He did not have to wait. Drago was waiting for him. They did not speak on the trip. The corporal's intuitive mechanism was aroused when coming in contact with Tatsuo. The underlying suspicion was not without merit. Too many odd things were happening of late in the war criminal stockade, such as the lights going out, the discovery that the switch had been pulled. Major Goto trying to escape again and the rice party on the pitcher's mound. Somehow Drago had the feeling Tatsuo's understanding of the English language gave him an edge on the workings in the stockade.

It's just too freaky, thought the corporal. *This guy and the rest of 'em have too much freedom. With the shit that's happening, someone's gotta know what's goin' on.*

This was Drago's first visit to the P.O.W. stockade. The compound held 5,000 Japanese of all ranks. The throng of men in the five-acre stockade sent out a constant buzz.

Sounds like a bee hive, thought the corporal.

Groups of soldiers were congregated throughout, some squatting, others walking in a transcendental state, while a few knelt with palms together in prayer; those praying bowed intermittently towards the sun.

Barbed wire enclosed the entire stockade; it was bisected every twenty yards by a tower, with a Marine manning a machinegun. The only gap in the camp was a path leading to the main gate where a Marine was posted in a shed. There were many lean-tos made of canvas held up by bamboo staves in the compound. In the center stood a huge tent the size of a field mess hall, where a large group of prisoners gathered. Inside, they milled about, or sat at makeshift tables playing various games, while others sat chatting. The buzz was stronger under the tent.

They reached the main gate; Drago gave the guard the release papers for Matsuki Ioto. The guard opened the gate. Tatsuo and Drago entered, Tatsuo in the lead.

As they walked, it became evident they were not welcome. They proceeded towards the large tent; the gathered groups parted for them. A few acknowledged Tatsuo with a slight bow, others who were making casual conversation stopped and glared at the corporal.

Tatsuo's eyes darted from one group to another. Tatsuo measured the corporal.

It is not right for the corporal to be here, he thought, *it is possible we could be in danger. Look at him, he is too calm. He is constantly scanning the area, his mind appears to be racing, He is far off, as though he were entering a schoolyard for the first time and measuring each individual as he goes.*

Tatsuo's military training under the major was so complete and intense it garnered respect for those of either side with the intuitive bravery of the ancients. To Tatsuo, the corporal measured up. Tatsuo's thoughts glided easily from his native culture to the period when he assimilated into American society while in the United

States. The melding occurred so effortlessly it startled him at times.

They entered the huge tent, and again the men gave way to Tatsuo and the corporal. In the center of the enclosure, a ten-foot-square floor was laid, resting a foot above the ground. A grossly huge man sat on a great chair of woven bamboo. The chair's back resembled a sun with spiked reeds, its rays flaring to the heavens; the scene was God enhanced. The man's girth left little of the seat showing, other than the blazing sun.

Buddha, thought Drago, *he looks like a statue of Buddha.*

The man sat as a king, with several men in attendance on either side of him. The Buddha's body had a triangular slope. His legs were the size of massive pine tree stumps. His body rose over his hips to a bloated yet firm midsection. His breasts lay on the bloat; shoulders, though huge, accentuated the triangle as it rose to a point above the man's head. His arms were extended, and his hands, palms open, rested on two tables. A full round face, with slits for eyes, measured the two coming towards him. A knot of pitch-black hair rose to the pinnacle of the triangle.

Tatsuo, when within ten feet of the sitting Buddha, turned to the corporal, bowed slightly, and motioned Drago to stop. Once he saw that Drago understood, he turned to the man on the platform. He walked forward a few feet and bowed, this time from the waist, in a subjugating manner. The Buddha raised his head in recognition of Tatsuo, and bowed his head ever so slightly.

"Speak to me, you buffoon, you who have brought this insignificant piece of dung into our presence," the Buddha snarled at Tatsuo.

"We are here to bring a Matsuki Ioto to the criminal stockade for questioning."

Drago folded his arms across his chest and glared at the Buddha.

That fucker could cut me in half, and eat a five course meal while watching me squirm. Hey, out there! Here's your war criminal, sitting up there. Come and get 'em!

Drago snickered. Some on the platform noticed. A bead of sweat emerged on Drago's upper lip.

The Buddha addressed his entourage.

"You see this tiny grub, this piss-eating scum, sneering at us? You see how far we have sunk? We will have to endure a slimy existence for surrendering to these maggots. Who knows this Matsuki Ioto?"

One of his charges raised his hand.

"Do not sit there; bring him here, you fool."

The man jumped up and left the tent.

They did not have to wait long; the Buddha's command was pure power. The man came back, dragging Matsuki with him. They both stood in front of their master and bowed from the waist. The Buddha moved his arm across his body to dismiss them, without looking up.

The three walked slowly out of the tent. Tatsuo and Drago, aware of the potency of the Buddha on the platform, sighed in relief when clear of the enclosure. Tatsuo's eyes surveyed the ground before him in submission. The corporal looked to the clear blue sky for solace. Their ward, Ioto, seemed oblivious to all around him.

Reunion

Drago noticed the scarcity of guards at the stockade. Beside the lone sentry at the gate, the only others were manning the towers. He scanned them; something drew him to one in particular. He shaded his eyes with his open palm and studied the tower. There was no mistaking Henry James, who was surveying the grounds from his perch. "Henry," Drago called out to him. "Henry, Henry James, what are you up to? It's me, Drago."

Henry James studied the forward area looking for the source of the voice.

"Henry, you old shit head, it's me. Over here!" Drago said, and waved his arms to get Henry's attention.

Drago's friend found him in a parted group of prisoners. He was about to wave to Drago when fear gripped him. Drago's waving of his arms made Henry mistakenly think his friend was in danger.

"I'll save ya, Drago, I'll save you!"

"What Henry? I don't get ya, what did you say?"

"I'll get you out of there," Henry said, and pulled back the bolt on the machine gun.

"No, no, Henry, that's not what's happening! It's okay, Henry."

Drago moved his arms more frantically in answer to Henry's plea.

"I won't let 'em touch ya," Henry yelled.

Drago befriended me. I won't let anyone hurt him. No one treated me like he did. I'll save him! Henry thoughts consoled him as he fired into the stockade.

"Jesus, Henry, no! Henry, no, oh my God!" he yelled, as men fell about him.

Tatsuo instinctively threw his body on the ground.
"Hiroshi was right," Tatsuo said out loud, "they will kill
us all, kill us all! I should have believed him. They are
dishonorable, these Americans."

Tatsuo would never understand, no matter how many
years he spent in the United States, the reason for the
destruction wrought in the camp that moment.

Men were screaming, blood was flowing, the ground
scarlet.

Henry's gun jammed. He pulled the bolt back with
force, and began firing again. Drago knew he could not
stop Henry from where he was. He bolted out of the
stockade past the posted guard at the gate. Marines were
rushing out of Quonset huts with armor of all description.
All headed for the stockade. As they ran they inserted clips
of ammunition into their rifles. They did not realize one of
their own was creating the carnage. When they reached
the perimeter of the stockade they lined up ready to stem
the uprising. With mouths agape they eyed the situation.

Drago mounted the tower. He jumped the first four
steps on the ladder in one bound, and then taking two
steps at a time he scaled to Henry's position. He forded the
railing, wrapped his arms around Henry, and threw him to
the floor of the tower. He held him there. Henry,
exhausted, did not resist. He knew it was his friend, the
Croat, who held him. The only person who had befriended
him. He smiled.

"See, I saved ya! I wouldn't let 'em do you any harm.
You're my friend."

Henry chuckled as Drago remembered him doing so
often. They were both calm, with Drago's arms still
holding Henry; they sat there among the expended shell
casings. Through the railing they watched the turmoil
below.

Tatsuo was not injured. He rose from the ground and stood there moving his head from side to side. With outstretched arms he blessed those that had fallen; with flexing fingers he called them to come to him. Tatsuo's eyes filled.

It is only retribution, he thought. *In Shanghai we lined up the prisoners, both British and Chinese, and summarily executed them.*

They are not disgraced any longer; they will not live to go home with heads bowed. It is the ascension that all of us hoped for. I wish that I met my fate here. It is as it should be; there are more dead than wounded. Their surrender is vindicated.

Henry sat quietly. Drago's heart was filled with anguish and despair wondering what would happen to Henry.

"Oh Jesus, Henry, what's gonna happen to ya now? If you had just waited we could have had a great reunion. Now look at this fuckin' mess, all because I made ya my friend, Henry!"

Drago held his breath to abate his sorrow. If he did not he would lose control.

One hundred Japanese were killed that afternoon. Only twenty were wounded. It was as Tatsuo said: Through death, vindication.

Tatsuo looked up at the tower. There he saw Henry and Drago. He honed in on the distraught Croatian. He smiled, his thoughts giving him satisfaction. The slaughter had breached a flaw in the corporal's armor.

Those of rank must not fall from the pedestal they have attained. The corporal gives into his emotions; it will cost him in times of stress.

Tatsuo, as all Japanese soldiers, related their own mores to those of their enemy.

The brass made up a tale. The veteran Henry, seeing the death of so many of his buddies, cracked. Henry James was not a combat veteran; he was only trying to save his friend, in the only way he knew how. A letter was sent apologizing to the Japanese officials in Tokyo; they filed it. No one understood the meaning of the letter.

Henry James was shackled to a flag pole outside the military police headquarters in Agana. They bound him with a straightjacket. Henry did not resist; after all, he saved his friend.

Tatsuo and Ioto waited for the corporal. They boarded the Jeep as truck loads of corpsmen arrived to attend to the wounded. No one spoke on the return trip. Tatsuo brushed past Drago as they parted. The contact seemed innocent enough, yet it was an action by Tatsuo, a subtle move denoting his disrespect for his captor. It would be repeated thousands of times in the future by the Japanese. The offence held no meaning for the Americans. This minute saving of face gave the Japanese hope for their future.

Loss of Face

Nakamura's pivotal loss of face involving Hiroshi had to be rectified; he had to regain his stature in the eyes of his subordinates. Somehow he had to reclaim what was lost: his command of the men in his sphere. Nakamura Toshio sought out Hiroshi and Akira.

"It is time we make a statement; our supplies are dwindling, we have consumed all the rations. We shall raid a village and secure the needed supplies there."

Hiroshi agreed; the K rations were all but gone. Since the supply depot was destroyed, the Americans had increased the guards at their previous caches. Two men walking posts were the order now. The remote villages would be their new source of supply.

They chose to raid the village where they were seen by the elders, which caused a series of events to be set in motion, culminating in a confrontation that Sgt. Nakamura had not foreseen.

Nakamura Toshio again called out the others; he wished to set a trap in the event more patrols were sent out. He garnered the grenades Hiroshi had stowed in his cave; they set off for the open area where the last battle ended. The enormous shell holes left them little room to set the trap. Toshio, after surveying the area, found a line of grass in the center extending clear across the open field. It would hide the wire connectors leading to the grenades. One end of the wires was attached to a tree trunk; the other end was staked directly across the field. Both grenades were secured to the stake and wire drawn through the pin. He instructed Hiroshi and Akira to sheer the grasses, and lay them on the wires. The trap set, they retired.

Hiroshi, while foraging for tubers, noticed a patrol. He sat quietly as the chattering Marines of Cpl. Paul's patrol passed him. He sought out Nakamura and Akira.

"They are totally unaware of our presence. They are completely unconcerned. Their superior is vigilant, but they pay him no heed," he told his two comrades.

Hiroshi was elated at the possibility of destroying such a small patrol. He reflected on their last foraging expedition, and meeting Tatsuo at the war criminal stockade. Tatsuo had been waiting for Hiroshi to appear. He wished to inform him of the incident at the Japanese stockade. Alone, returning to the mess tent with the empty pot, Hiroshi called out to him. Tatsuo was elated and quickly joined his comrade.

"It is good to see you, Hiroshi." Tatsuo slapped Hiroshi on his shoulder. "It is like you said: they will kill us all."

He told him of the murder at the stockade.

"Aieee, it is true, like I said, they lie! They are dishonorable curs." Tatsuo's relating the massacre at the P.O.W. stockade primed Hiroshi to retaliate against the Americans.

"My position is suspect here since your last visit. They have posted a guard on our quarters; we must be accounted for every evening. There is talk of us being shackled. Who knows? The burly sergeant has bolted the switch on the electric current. We wait for the typhoons to appear for the major to try his escape. The storms cause confusion, and then the opportunity may arise again. It is all we can hope for. The major and I will join you if escape is possible." Hiroshi beamed at Tatsuo's declaration.

Each respectfully bowed to the other, and went on their way.

~~~~~~~~~~~~~~~~

Nakamura Toshio, Hiroshi, and Akira followed the Marines as they walked along the river bed. They waited in the cover of the jungle while the patrol passed through a valley leading to the first rise. The foliage being sparse, they moved with caution. The three renegades sat on the first rise, viewing the Marines as they approached the second hill to the beach.

How foolish they are, thought Nakamura. *They make no effort to conceal their position.*

The exhausted Marines peeled off their equipment and stacked their rifles in the slight depression on the top of the hill. Sgt. Nakamura instructed his men on where and how they would approach the patrol. On a signal from Toshio, they would broach the summit and fire their weapons.

Nakamura signaled and Hiroshi and Akira fired, he then fired at the third man, then turned his weapon on the stunned leader and fired again. He drew Cpl. Paul's bayonet and cut the man's throat.

They gathered all the equipment, stripped the dead of their clothing and disappeared into the jungle. As they retreated, Toshio Nakamura's mind raced, haunted as always by his confused feelings of dread when taking a life.

Why do I feel this dread? He questioned. *I go to the mountains and am at peace. I watch the animals moving about and am happy watching their mischief and foraging. It would hurt me to kill any of God's creatures in the forests. How is it I must do damage and death to another human? My Emperor tells me it is good to kill the infidel. The Westerners have exploited us from the beginning of their intrusion into our sphere. We kill them as readily as we murder others of our own race. It is perplexing. Each deed has a value all its own. Extracting a blooming flower: is it worth more than a human life? Through it all I must survive. I have no hate, yet I kill. I have saved face with this last endeavor.*

Hiroshi walked behind Nakamura and wondered about him. The sergeant was warranted by the Emperor; he must have merit. Still, there were many contradictions about Sergeant Nakamura. Yet the task now completed gave some credence to their superior's worth.

We have just vindicated some of our comrades by destroying the Marines on the hill. We shall do more damage, Hiroshi's thoughts raced. Though we will be hunted again, we are well hidden. We are the Emperor's guardians.

Hiroshi had strange feelings about the attack on the hill. While killing the Americans, he felt elated. It was an ecstatic experience, creating a physical high from the adrenaline generated. Generally, the feeling passed if you survived. That need for the ancients to possess his body through stealth did not abate this time. The electric, elated feeling stayed with him, coming close to the feeling of a sexual rush. He remembered the same thing happening as he stood precariously on a cliff edge beside a waterfall 200 feet high. His toes on the fringe of the abyss, flexing his body up and forward, he felt the ground giving way. He then raised his arms and flapped them to regain his balance. It was the power of mind and body exemplified. The power he attained in destroying a human being felt glorious. Though he did not know it, he shared the same sensations with Major Goto.

I have not had this happen before; it is frightening in its intensity, yet quite enjoyable. They deserved to die, those misfits! Their souls will remain stagnant for eons. But the glory of it will wane. I will seek to relive the experience again, when another opportunity arises to eradicate other of their ilk I will be ready. He savored the thought.

Major Goto

Major Goto realized his rage had been his undoing. He made a decision to try and outwit his captors in new ways, which meant he had to suppress his anger and control his emotions. He would begin by groveling. He remembered the prisoners in China, close to eradication, as they begged him for mercy. It had angered him. He unleashed his rage as he sliced the beggars into eternity. He would put aside the shame of cowering, and outwit his jailers.

The cell door opened and Tatsuo stood there with his meal. The guard, ever on the alert when dealing with the major, was stunned as Major Goto, on bended knee, bowed in front of him. He told others of the major's apparent submission. The vigilance slackened. All were deceived by his ploy. His actions gave Tatsuo more freedom in their interaction. From then on, they conversed freely. The wily major continued to beg his captors for absolution.

~~~~~~~~~~~~~~~

Major Goto's remembered the start of his training when he stood before his Sensei with aggression in his heart, and bowed to the person who had bested him in every encounter. His instructor was the only adversary ever to defeat the then Lieutenant Goto; all others fell to him. The Sensei's dominance unnerved him, and tormented his soul.

Sent to China in an infantry unit, ancestral privilege took precedence. One of the Samurai, they placed him in regimental intelligence. Interrogation of prisoners challenged the lieutenant: torture was the extracting force, cooperation was the result. Once the information flowed and there was no further need for the prisoner, he would be executed. Here was where Goto first succumbed to the elation created by the taking of life. His sword eventually became an instrument delivering the God-enhanced euphoria of knowing the power of life or death lay within him. Severing the head of a person from his body required practice. Lieutenant Goto, with every execution, adapted various methods of decapitation; he studied the neck of each individual prior to taking the sword from its scabbard. Evaluating the thickness or the length of the neck determined whether a single stroke would send the head out and away from the body. Thick or short, Goto's proficiency in cleaving cleanly became legendary.

For a time, Goto did not participate in actual combat. His skill at extracting information from prisoners kept him at headquarters. But he wished to display his prowess on the battlefield. Like his Samurai ancestors, he excelled in all the martial arts.

While in China, during an exercise of hand-to-hand combat, a low-ranking Korean soldier bested the lieutenant. The soldier's knowledge of *Taekkyeon* overpowered Goto. The ancient art of *Taekkyeon* was banned in Korea by the Japanese. On discovering the soldier's proficiency in the art, he should have been executed. Goto saved the man from execution and ordered the soldier to instruct him in this ancient art. Hour after hour he faced the soldier, until his mastery was acknowledged by the Korean, while lying in pain on the ground. The Korean bowed low to the lieutenant; Goto, satisfied, called off the training. He then had the man executed.

When the lieutenant first engaged in an action involving his regiment, he came to the realization all his training in the martial arts was useless in the face of an armed enemy. His great body strength did not frighten a person aiming a rifle at him 500 yards away. A rifle bullet did not adhere to the rules of unarmed combat.

Finally placed in command of a company, he brilliantly outflanked the enemy, causing a frenzied retreat. As a reward, he was sent home to Japan to the 1st Kurine Reserve Officer's School and promoted to the rank of captain. Because of his proficiency in Judo, Karate, swordsmanship, and bayonet fencing, he was given the honor of instructing hand-to-hand combat. He and his pupils excelled. He was promoted to major.

After leaving the academy, he was assigned to command a regiment slated to invade the American protectorate of Guam; it would be the first American territory to capitulate to the forces of Imperial Japan. After securing the surrender of the main garrison, it was his duty to prepare the defense of the island. Setting this aside, he led patrols to flush out the few remaining Americans in outlying areas who refused to surrender. When cornered by overwhelmingly superior forces, the Americans surrendered. The major, angered by this, branded them cowards, and used that excuse to execute them, temporarily satiating his blood lust.

~~~~~~~~~~~~~~~

As Goto waited in the War Criminal Stockade for an opportunity to escape, he exercised his neck, arms, shoulders, and legs by flexing them under the restraints the Marines put on him. He knew simulating attack and defensive moves would strengthen him for the day when he could attack his jailers.

~~~~~~~~~~~~~~

Two days of clear skies, a soft breeze filled the air. A typhoon, 400 miles away, sucked the moisture out of the air to gain strength in its movement towards Guam. The typhoon season was about to begin. The Marines brought the six-by-six Internationals into the stockade. Their chain winches were crisscrossed over the Quonsets that held the prisoners. The Marines abandoned their tents, as they would be torn from their moorings easily when the torrential rains started. The mess hall, a Quonset, would be their home for a week; it was also secured by the mighty trucks.

~~~~~~~~~~~~~~

The major was still bound by the straightjacket. Tatsuo had a knife for slicing meat that supplemented the prisoners' rice. He snapped the point off the blade, and proceeded to hone it on a flat stone. It became razor sharp. He placed it in his superior's bowl of rice, and spooned it into his mouth. The major was not surprised. They had discussed the action earlier. They planned the escape to coincide with the advent of the typhoons.

The major now faced a choice. If he saw a chance to escape, he would use the blade to release himself from the restraints and slip into the jungle to a prearranged spot, where Tatsuo would be waiting for him. If the opportunity did not arise, he would commit *Seppuku* in his cell. If he did succeed, he would join the others, and they would be a formidable avenging force.

The Threat

Hiroshi and Akira moved leisurely down a path when they came upon two water buffalo grazing. Hiroshi and Akira shouted, the buffalos turned from them and tore through the undergrowth. The buffalos' panic increased as briars tore at their eyes and coats. They bleated in pain and rage. They exited where the Marine patrol, with Juarez in the lead, traversed their escape route. The animals galloped down the path. Marines and weapons flew in an effort to escape or be trampled by the beasts.

Hiroshi and Akira gazed through the gaping hole in the maze of briars, watching as men and weapons were scattered by the rampaging buffalo. Fear of discovery sent them scurrying. Reversing their path, they made for their cave, where they stayed.

Eventually the Marines neared their hideout. Hiroshi motioned for Akira to be quiet. The patrol stopped. An officer, after conferring with a huge dark-skinned man, moved to inspect the cave. The renegades cowered deep in the cave. The authority, hands on hips, looked up at the opening, then turned and again spoke to the dark-skinned man. They continued on their way, past the opening. Hiroshi watched as the last man in line came into view; it was Cpl. Drago from the War Criminal Stockade, who removed a grenade from his pocket and moved closer to the opening.

Hiroshi thought, *He is about to throw a grenade into our midst; we're doomed.*

Earlier, Hiroshi and Akira had scavenged pieces of a destroyed tank and stored them in the cave. Thinking quickly, they snatched a metal plate from the wreckage and placed it in front of their position in the cave, to absorb any exploding grenade fragments.

Hiroshi was relieved as he watched Drago relent and return the grenade into a pocket in his fatigues.

Ah, so that is the second time I have viewed this man that Tatsuo warned me about, He thought. *Just like at the criminal stockade, he did not follow through as a warrior should and destroy us. There is no challenge here as Tatsuo predicted; I will be victorious if we finally meet. A soldier must follow his instincts. Why does he so often relent?*

Hiroshi, like others of his kind, would never understand the American psyche. The Americans played at cowboys and Indians and cops and robbers in their youth. Their killing was done through cunning, yet all walked away unharmed. Christian ethic forbids the taking of life. The fear of retribution in the ever-after stymied their instantaneous response, resulting in many of their deaths in combat. Those that set aside that belief often fared better in combat, but were seen as callous by their brethren in arms. The callous ones left religion and ethics behind and survived.

Hiroshi and Akira left the cave after the Marines passed. They scoured the jungle off the trails for an area where they would not be likely to come into further contact with the Marines on patrol.

~~~~~~~~~~~~~~

Nakamura Toshio was oblivious to the new threat. Staying in his dugout during the day, he knew nothing of the patrol. He was preoccupied with skinning a rat he caught in a snare. That evening, he went to the river to fill his canteens and was caught in an unexpected ambush. A bullet broke skin on his arm. After fleeing, he sat knowing he was not pursued. He recalled an incident in Manchukuo that terrified him: A Japanese soldier, captured by the communists, screamed into the night while being tortured. Nakamura imitated the screams he heard; he hoped it would send fear to the Americans as it had to his people there. He was not wrong; all of the patrol thought the chilling cry was one of their own being tortured. There was general concern by some, and the release of bodily fluids by others. Nakamura went back to his sanctuary, unnerved.

~~~~~~~~~~~~~~

Hiroshi heard the scream; it upset him and Akira. He wondered if one of their own was being tortured, making the fearsome cry.

Yes, someone else has discovered the patrol. Is the discoverer in danger, or is he preying on the minds of the oppressors? It is not new, this way of driving fear into the enemy; it is as old as the Samurai. With every swing of the blade an adrenaline-induced utterance of great magnitude is emitted, striking fear into those within earshot. They will not run, these Americans. I have seen disorder in the Chinese, where thousands fled the imperial armies. Here on this speck in the giant ocean no one gives quarter. So be it.

~~~~~~~~~~~~~~

The next morning, Nakamura, secure in his refuge, thought about the night before and its consequences. It had been a large patrol. It was not safe to move about in the jungle. He felt lethargic; the events seemed to extract more of his energy, add more stress than usual. When he finally made it to his home in the jungle, a nervous spasm engulfed him. He felt feverish. Alternating blasts of cold and heat contorted his frame. He reached for relief in prayer. He knelt, and with palms together, bowing, repeating the primary phrases that tended to alleviated the ferment that gripped him. Eventually, he relaxed. When the spasm subsided, he rationalized his condition, blaming his state on a fever. The other alternative, fear, he discounted and placed in the extreme depths of his subconscious.

Peace came to him; he slept. The sound of exploding American grenades woke him and renewed his spasms.

He would not leave his dugout; he would leave the investigation to Hiroshi. *Patrols will increase*, he thought. He pressed his body to the wall of his self-induced prison, then picked up a chisel he had formed from a sheet of metal and commenced to shred a coconut. When finished, he sat back and sighed.

Book 3

Destiny

Scorpions and Typhoons—November 1946

The typhoons were relentless in the fall of 1946. Quonsets were torn from their moorings, set down on top of other Quonsets; no one, nothing was safe. During the first storm, Drago's gun section was awakened when the roof of their quarters peeled off. They left, treading through six inches of water, while equipment and all manner of gear floated towards the entrance of their hut.

As all good Marines, they took with them nothing but their rifles, and made their way to the winched-down mess hall. They would spend four days there, until the deluge subsided.

Juarez left Drago just as the second typhoon reached Guam. Drago entered the jungle at the head of the Talofofo river basin, then settled down between two trees to wait out the storm. The rain became torrential. Winds flailed the undergrowth, grasses hissed and danced. Drago cursed. His poncho was left behind; the rain gear would have added a bit of comfort. There was no relief.

The river rose and Drago decided to move to higher ground. His quest for a safe haven brought him to an overhang deep enough on the lee side of a hill to afford him protection.

Debris flew in all direction; trees were uprooted, and, like tooth-picks, went sailing on the unrelenting wind. The fierce storm took his breath away. Breathing itself became hazardous; the dense humidity displaced needed oxygen. The wind tore at his face and body. Stinging sand and minute particles of vegetation invaded his sanctuary. Large debris slammed the outer wall of the enclosure.

Scorpions rest in dark caverns to immobilize prey. They sting; the venom does its work quickly. Intrusion of their lair is considered a threat. Drago, in an effort to avoid the torrent outside pressed his body to the wall of the overhang. He dislodged a scorpion; it fell on his hand, its tail arched over its body, striking. He quickly threw off the scorpion. The damage was done. In minutes his hand became swollen; the venom raced through his bloodstream.

A fever engulfed him. He tried to think of a solution, searching his mind for answers, for something he learned in training. He found nothing. The venom trapped him.

The corporal's state became dream-like, hallucinations intruded. He spoke to the walls; there was no response. He passed out.

Dreams raced through his mind, single vignettes fluttered and faded away. His mother came to him, her hands on his face, laughing, telling tales of his grandfather, the Serb. She told him stories of his greatness in battle, told of the medals he received from the great King of Serbia. He and the other Serbs deserted the Austro-Hungarian Army, leaving their ranks on the Russian front. She told him of his father being flogged for the desertion of the Serbs, his grandfather under his command, a catalyst in the insurrection.

"*Slushi*, listen," his mother said as she disclosed his father's disgrace. She looked around, fearing that the old grenadier might have overheard her.

"Your *Deda*, grandfather, fell in love with a horse so much, he stole it. He had to give up his home in Ponchovo on the Serb side of the Danube; he would not give up the horse. He came to live in our town in Hungary. They could not come to fetch him there. A horse thief, he could not return to his native land. The Army took him. He was fighting in the Ukraine. All the Serbs bolted over to the Russians side. You must understand, Serbs do not fight against their own kind, their desertion rational in their eyes, Slushi." Again she looked about to see if the grenadier was listening.

His mother faded away from view. A tintype appeared. Drago saw a gnarled old man, face pock-marked, with full moustache and long grey side burns on a stern face. He wore an army fore-and-aft hat with an oval tricolor pin, representing the Army of Serbia. The face came alive.

"*Kakos ta ve moy Hervarti*," said the gnarled apparition.

"This young Croat is ill, my *Deda*," answered Drago.

" *Ocha da ida, na moi da plachahs.*"

"No grandfather, I will not cry, but I am afraid my sickness will not go away."

"It will go away. *Slushi moy sin.* I will tell you of my adventure. When we gave ourselves over to the Rushkys they did not know what to do with us. Confusion reigned when the Bolsheviks gained power. *Stoy ouda, na moy da idash.* Stay here. Do not go away. I will tell you more."

"We walked a thousand miles and more to the port of St. Petersburg on the Baltic Sea. There we boarded a big boat, two thousand of us. We were to cross the Baltic Sea, and around the isle of the British."

"As many as could went to the life boats. It was cold. The chance of getting through was impossible; the German U boats controlled the sea. *Taka yah, Boga nas chuvie.* God watched over us. *Taka yeh.*"

"We passed north of the isle of the British then into the Irish Sea. We followed the coast of France and Spain. We went through the Straits of Gibraltar, and saw the Great Mont Gibraltar. Then through the Mediterranean Sea to Constantinople, where the Turks fired on us. Then we went to Saloniki in Greece; there we joined the rest of the displaced Serbian Army. *Boga pomosi nas.* God helped us. We fought the Germans there from cave to cave up the mountain side. The Germans were ferocious, the Turks ran from us.

"The tools given to me by God to survive were a fire that could not be put out; it caused me much pain. I turned against my brethren. Your mother has not told you of the end of my life. I killed my brother over a piece of pork. Others in my clan put out the fire in me for fear I would turn on them.

"I give you my spirit, the spirit of the greatest of kings, that of the warrior. Take care, Drago; your quest may engulf you. I give you my knowledge of survival; it is in you, a spirit hidden for when you have the need to call on it. *Boga pomosi, yah idam.*"

"Goodbye grandfather. I heed your words. *Yah chuvum.*"

The fever subsided, as did the apparition. Drago did not know how long he had been captive to his delirium. His strength was sapped.

The storm had exhausted itself; a cool breeze entered his shelter. He drank and ate from his supply, and then he slept peacefully. Three days he slept. He gained his strength; it was time to continue his quest.

Akira and Hiroshi's Trial

Hiroshi and Akira braved the storm in their cave. The river rose high enough to put them in peril. There was no escape. They had to risk the raging river. Akira was the first to engage the frenzied Talofofo. He was swept away. Hiroshi clung precariously to the lip of the cave, watching Akira disappear.

I will surely die if I let go; I cannot swim! The wind tore him loose and into the wild river. Willingly he accepted his fate. Hitting his head on a rock as he propelled down the swollen river, he was knocked unconscious. A single forked branch denied him the accepted glory of death, by pinning him just above the torrent.

~~~~~~~~~~~~~~~~

Akira flailed as the river carried him; it deposited him on the sand beach leading to the sea. Both sea and river vied for his life. He crawled to higher ground, groped his way to a stand of grasses, and buried himself there as the typhoon thrashed about him. The pounding rain chilled him to the bone. He brought his legs up and entwined his arms about them. He buried his head in the pocket created by his fetal position. Uncontrollable chattering teeth sent out a rat-tat-tat, hypnotically pulling Akira into a trance. He sat in that stupor. Descending deeper, his salvation was the packet that held a photo of his wife, daughter and son. With entwined fingers he embraced the photo; its warmth carried him through his trial. There he sat until the storm abated. On the third day, quiet invaded the land; the storm's wrath left a vacuum that cleared the air.

He moved to the beach, where he evaluated his position. As a subordinate, he was left with few decisions. He would follow and submit to the whims of those in his company; so the Emperor had ordained. His participation in the actions taken left him ambivalent. What would happen if they were captured? Would he be subject to immediate execution for his killing of the Americans that had entered their sanctuary? If he surrendered, would he be placed in one of the camps that now held thousands of his comrades, as Tatsuo described?

The only alternative was to follow in his superiors' footsteps, until other decisions were made for him by fate or the American force. His free will was constantly controlled by other factors. It put him at odds with his need to survive and see his family again. At times, he thought of deserting this beggared existence by simply going over to the Americans. The memory of those killed by the Marines when surrendering warned him that they, too, could deny him his goal of returning to his family. He was in constant turmoil, yet he never let his feeling be known to the others.

On occasions when he was sent on a mission alone and free of their dominance, he would summon thoughts of home. The waterlogged conditions on Guam evoked a mirrored vision of terraced rice paddies sloping on a hillside. Glistening, tiny sprouts raised their crowns above the mirrored crests. Each sprout tickled by soft breezes sent out circular rivulets, testaments to the life of the plants.

He felt the sun bathing him in its warmth. He longed to see his native land again. The longing stimulated his nerve endings; combined with his memories the impulses spread from the back of his head up and over his eyes where tears poured down his cheeks. In his mind, Akira summoned the child with open arms, the child's glee when seeing his father echoed Akira's feelings; he embraced the boy. Akira smiled at the memory as he sat alone.

As was customary, his wife had been chosen for him. The union was brokered by their parents. Akira had a captivating smile. When the young girl first saw the man with the bright smile in the flat round face, his eyes disappearing in the throes of his stimulating wide grin, her knees buckled at the thought of being his wife. Love filled her heart that day, never diminishing.

There would be no reunion. B29 bombers left Guam on the evening of July 19th, 1945 to raid Osaka, where his wife and children were on holiday. They were caught in a firestorm. They perished together as the fire sucked air from their bodies to feed the storm.

~~~~~~~~~~~~~~~

Hiroshi gained consciousness long enough to assess his condition.

The blackness that enveloped me was a glorious gift from God. It is sad that I could not be received in that manner in the heavens. It would be better than the pain I feel in my head now. He moaned. His subconscious released demons that he would later have to grapple with. He spoke to his father in the dream state.

~~~~~~~~~~~~~~~

"Father, I wish better for myself. I have proven my worth in my studies. I have shown physical prowess on the athletic field. I have watched the Samurai in training, and seen men fall before them. In my heart, I know that I would not be defeated if the opportunity was given to me. But, because of my low breeding, I must grovel."

"Silence, my son. I, a lowly cobbler, have found my place in life."

"Father, I have been faithful to our cause and suffered hardships without whimpering. With these hands, I have destroyed the enemy. It is not easy for me to watch as those less deserving have gained the status of which I am worthy."

"It is your duty to serve and not dishonor your family. You have done well," said his father. "Our place requires that we bow in submission to our betters. So be it."

"I have no betters," Hiroshi countered.

Escape

The war criminal stockade was battered by the storm. One of the towers toppled over onto the concertina wire. The Marine standing watch on that tower flew forward onto the flooded ground, landing in a puddle, two feet short of the first cell block.

The Quonsets strained under the winches. The guards were ordered to bring the prisoners to the secured mess hall; there they would be shackled and guarded until the storm subsided.

The storm's power made movement perilous; it slammed Marines against the cell block walls.

Sergeants Perlas and Braxton secured a rope at the mess hall, then crawled with it to the cell blocks. They wrapped the rope around the posts holding up the tin overhang attached to the Quonset huts. Two Marines were then chosen to bring in the prisoners. On the first attempt, the chosen Marines were battered with a piece of flying sheet metal. Stunned and lacerated, they fought their way back.

Corporal Flint, his arm in a cast, went out fearlessly, dragging two privates with him. He cleared seven of the eight cell blocks, then fell exhausted on the mess hall floor. Sergeant Perlas went out to bring in the remainder of the prisoners.

Major Goto was the last to be extricated. He spent his time well. Using his feet, he placed the knife tip into a groove in the floorboard, the sharp end protruding. He maneuvered his back over it, and shredded the straight-jacket. He was free. Still wearing the shredded restraint, he braced his back against the rear of the cell.

The cell door opened; two privates entered. Goto rushed them. At the door, he took a stand, shooting both arms out from the frayed jacket, slamming the privates against the cell walls. The two guards would never forget the attack. The major's fist, gnarled and hardened from constant training in the martial arts, struck each private in the chest, fracturing both of their breast-bones.

Perlas stood directly in front of the cell block; Goto used the force of the attack to thrust his body forward. Perlas was knocked down by the major as he ran. He lay on the ground, stunned, and hesitated long enough for the major to gain momentum in his flight. He regained his senses as fast as he could, hoping to counter-strike the major.

Major Goto ran, the wind at his back; he strode in air. It carried him ten feet before his feet touched the ground. He sprang again and repeated the action. Three times he was carried by the lashing wind, ending at the perimeter of the stockade. With one more burst of power, the wind surged upward, carrying him over the wire displaced by the fallen tower.

He shouted out, "I am flying! The ancients' divine wind gives me strength to surmount all before me. The kamikaze is strong in my spirit."

As he flew with outstretched arms, from his innards he growled out that fearsome adrenaline-induced cry of the Samurai. Perlas watched, fascinated by the major's flight. Goto landed on a bed of rain-flattened grasses, cushioning his fall. He ran off, laughing.

A Cocoon and Denial

Nakamura's dugout flooded. He had to leave. Taking only a rope, he went searching for a sturdy palm tree. Palms, he knew, held up to strong winds. Finding one with a sturdy trunk, he ran the rope around the base and then tied it around his waist. Shimmying up with his hands and feet, he climbed the tree. Both he and the tree were battered by the wind. He needed all his strength to reach the foliage above. Finally reaching the palm fronds, he secured the rope tightly to his perch and burrowed in among them. Deep into the fronds he was sheltered from the rain and wind. Nakamura's capacity to disengage body and soul from danger served him well; he drifted into a comatose state.

~~~~~~~~~~~~~~~

Tatsuo followed the witnesses. As the Marines were herding them into the huge mess hall, an opportunity arose; he darted into the jungle. He and Major Goto had prearranged a place to meet if he escaped; it was directly in line with the fallen tower. The wind's strength drove him to the ground; he grasped the vegetation there and held on. He crawled to the road. He had to pass over it to reach his destination. Standing upright, he sprinted across. The wind gusted and slammed into his back.

Debris flew everywhere. A flying two-by-four ripped from its mooring, nails exposed, struck Tatsuo with such force the board tore his calf muscle as neatly as a butcher slices a hind quarter of beef. His aspirations of revenge were quelled by the force of the typhoon. He would be found, after the typhoon passed, and sent to the naval hospital. They gave him a pair of crutches that would be his constant companion for the rest of his life.

Perlas and Goto

Sergeant Perlas's need to apprehend Goto was set aside as he went to the aid of the two Marines struck down by Major Goto. Both were writhing in pain. After he tended them as best he could, Perlas ran to the mess hall and found Braxton. He pulled him aside.

"He got away," he told the sergeant.

"Who got away?" Braxton questioned.

"That piss-pot major. He hit the two guys with me; they're real bad off. We have to get some help for them."

Braxton scanned the enclosure; he found a navy corpsman sipping coffee. He went to him.

"You have to go out there and take care of the men that got clobbered by that fuckin' Jap major."

"I ain't goin' out there! No sir, not me, you could get killed out there," said the corpsman.

"Listen to me, you shithead, you do what I tell you, or I'll kick the shit outta ya right here and now. Do you understand?"

"OK, Sarge! Where are they?"

"Follow that rope outside. You'll find them in the last cell block."

The corpsman went off. As he moved along the rope he spoke to himself.

Dummy, you don't fuck around with Braxton. No sir, he never blows his top. You saw the look on his face; that's enough, you dumb fuck. He ranted on, his fear of the storm less than his fear of Sgt. Braxton.

Perlas and Braxton went off to find Lt. Warren. Nothing could be done without consulting their superior. They found him outside the door to the mess hall, watching the storm. The lieutenant reveled in the turmoil.

The sergeants informed him of the escaped major.

"Nothin' ya can do now, boys. We'll have to wait till this dies down, then go after his ass."

~~~~~~~~~~~~~~~

Major Goto sprinted out of view of the stockade. He clung to some small saplings, but the wind tore him free. Crawling, he reached the river bed. The major lowered himself into the churning water. He laced his arms through a protrusion of roots left bare by the rushing river. An overhang of earth hid him from view. He submerged himself up to his chin. There, he waited out the storm.

~~~~~~~~~~~~~~~

Major Goto's escape plagued Sgt. Perlas. *I gotta do something,* he fretted. *This is crazy; with the start that Jap has, we'll never get him back into the stockade.*

He again searched out the lieutenant. He found him where they last left him, watching the storm.

"Look, sir, there's a loose truck that I'd like to take out to our base in Agana, pick up our gun crews, and have 'em here when this thing is over. That way we can start hunting Goto right away. The guys we have here have to keep an eye on the rest of these birds. Unless we bring the others here, we're really up shit's creek."

"It's a bitch out there, Perlas."

"Yeah, but those trucks are such brutes; it don't mean nothin'."

"OK, let's go."

"Now wait a minute, Lieutenant. You sure that's what you want to do?"

"Hot damn, Sergeant. You think I'm gonna let you have all that fun all by yourself? Damned if I will. Besides, I have to take the responsibility for this. I can't lay it on you all. Let's go."

They sped down the highway. As big as the truck was, the wind blew it from side to side along the road. It was of no consequence; there was no one else travelling there. Debris smashed against the windshield. A twirling piece of pipe speared through the windshield and imbedded itself in the seat between them.

"Jesus, my savior, you done it again! God bless me, he brought me good luck again. God bless! How'd you like that Perlas?"

Perlas took one hand off the steering wheel, and gently stroked the imbedded pipe.

"Ya never know, just plain luck, sure as hell." Perlas said.

They picked up the gun crews after talking to the new commander, Col. Kramer. The colonel's knowledge of the lieutenant's record held back any questions he might have asked. The storm subsided during the drive back to the stockade.

~~~~~~~~~~~~~~

The storm finally passed, leaving the air clean. Fierceness, now gone, was replaced by a penetrating silence. Nothing moved. All through the island, stillness pervaded. The quiet created an anxious feeling of dread. In the typhoon's aftermath, the stillness held all in limbo.

Hiroshi's Search

Hiroshi woke and realized he was pinned to the fork in the tree. He extricated his body with great effort; it exhausted him. The river was receding. He fell to the river bank, and lay there. The nauseating pain in his head would not end; again he lapsed into a fevered sleep. He awoke, restored, and went off to find Akira.

As he trudged along the riverbed, he thought, *Akira, I must find Akira. I wonder if the river killed him. I must find him.* He felt a stirring in his genitals. He looked about as a child would at being discovered in the act of masturbation.

He followed the river bank as it flowed to the sea. There, he found Akira. They sat together, not saying a word, both singularly at ease, knowing they would not have to travel alone. The gift that God gave them through association became more apparent to Hiroshi. Again a welling in his groin surprised him; it was fleeting, and passed. He thoughtlessly embraced Akira. His companion was taken aback. Hiroshi, realizing his action made Akira uncomfortable; he withdrew and playfully slapped him on his back. They laughed, Akira nervously.

Drago waited until the river subsided, then went out to inspect the cave. He approached it with care, and patiently waited to see if it was occupied. There was no activity, so he crawled up and entered. Finding the empty K ration containers, he knew that the cave had recently been occupied. Not wanting to sound an alarm, he left the containers where they were. As he left the cave, he noticed his boot had left an imprint in the softened path.

Drago loosened his shoelaces and broke off some reeds growing there; he tied the reeds to the bottom of his boots, thereby eliminating any further imprints. He erased the disturbed earth with a handful of reeds, leaving no sign of his presence.

He moved off and sat in the same area that the patrol occupied when they first went out to find the renegades. He remembered when his group of replacements first arrived on Guam. Back then, he had talked with a veteran, a Sgt. Sorenson. Sorensen was with the 9th Defense Battalion, before it became known as the 9th Triple A Battalion. From Guadalcanal, then to New Georgia, and finally settling on Guam, Sorensen was lauded as a great tracker. Back then, Drago shared a beer with him and Sorenson's friend, Cpl. Connelly. Drago listened to him with great interest. "You can smell 'em out there," Sorensen stated. "They put this gook on themselves. They take it from the river; smear it on to keep the bugs off. Ya sniff 'em, and as the scent gets stronger, the closer they are to you. Smell like a rancid swamp, they do. That's it, a stinkin' swamp.

"They're pretty regular, they are, and use the same paths every day. Everywhere they've been we had to root them out. There aren't any dumb ones out there. They adjust well, they're a cagy bunch a bastards.

"We sure killed a lot of people. Some of the natives on the island weren't supposed to be out there; they got killed too. We killed anything that moved. When headquarters Fleet Marines said the island was secured, the division left the rest to us; secured my ass.

"We killed a lot a people. Lost some, but killed a lot. We've been doin' this since Guadalcanal, hoppin' from island to island." Sorensen finished his beer and walked out of the tent.

"Best fuckin' Marine I ever saw, that Sorenson," said Connelly while holding up a tent pole. "Nobody holds a candle to him. There hasn't been a patrol he hasn't volunteered for. He can spot an ambush by signs none of us ever see. He is some fuckin' Marine." With that statement, Cpl. Connelly left the tent.

Drago remembered Sorenson's words. He wondered if he would measure up; to do what he had to do.

Taking to heart what Sorenson said, Drago followed the path along the river bank, noting the packed, slick mud where the Japanese had walked. It led him around the Jap regiments' last stand on the outskirts of the jungle. He followed it further and came to the point where the water buffalo stampeded; following that path brought him back to the cave.

Rather than being plagued by mosquitoes, gnats and other flying pests, Drago dug into the river bed and spread the putrid mud all over his exposed body parts. The marauders now buzzed around and about him looking for that one place not smeared by the gook. It was futile; the corporal was undisturbed.

Retracing his steps, he sat on a little knoll looking out over the booby-trapped field. From there, he could scan the whole battleground. To his front, he could see a small break in the perimeter of the jungle where they had to pass to circumvent the open ground. He sat and mulled over the situation. *I can get them from here*, he thought. *They just got to give me a shot. They travel just like rabbits bein' pushed, goin' in a full circle. I'll wait 'em out.*

Assessment

Hiroshi and Akira sat on the sand and absorbed the quiet in awe. The two Japanese had their contemplation disturbed by a revving motor. The spell was broken by a six-by-six International truck speeding down the road. They sprinted to the nearby jungle and hid.

Needing food, they went off again, skirting the jungle just off the road. The path before them would take them to the Marine supply depot. As they followed the fringe of the jungle, they came across another tributary of the Talofofo River, which rewarded them with a case of C rations imbedded in the mud. They sat and ate ravenously, ingesting handfuls of beans and bacon and plum pudding. They lay on their backs like slugs, unable to move. As evening approached, they decided to rest and return to their cave in the morning.

When morning came, they wrapped their cache in their clothing, and slung the packages over their foreheads, the bulk resting on their backs.

~~~~~~~~~~~~~~

Nakamura woke in the silence and left his refuge in the palm fronds. Returning to his dugout, he bailed it out, then spread reeds on the floor to absorb the remaining moisture. Two shrimp traps hung high above the floor. All others had been washed away by the storm.

His concern for the safety of Hiroshi and Akira gnawed at him. He had seen neither of them since the typhoon began. As soon as he organized the remainder of his belongings, he would search them out. He feared for their safety. An M1 rifle lay hidden in a crevice above the water line, taken from the Marines on the hill. He inspected it, and found it in working order. That pleased him. He would take it with him.

Drago's vigil was interrupted by a sow and her piglets. The sow squealed upon seeing the corporal. He turned his head in their direction; they fled.

He scanned the area for about two hours; it proved to be tedious. The jungle opened up about one hundred yards in front of Drago's position. A shadow moving between trees there caught his eye. As he put the stock of the rifle to his shoulder, Hiroshi appeared. Drago couldn't get a shot off before Hiroshi disappeared into the foliage. He cursed under his breath, but held fast to the same point, and was rewarded when Akira shuffled into the open area, huffing under his load.

"Gotcha," Drago said, and fired.

The shot tore through the cans of C rations on Akira's back. He stopped and looked about to see where the bullet came from.

Fool, thought Drago. *He should have kept movin'. I've got 'em now.*

But Akira disappeared before Drago could get off another shot.

Akira, running down the path, threw his load into the jungle. His fear was so intense it blocked any sensible action; he kept running.

"Imbecile," Hiroshi said as Akira passed him, "Get off the path!"

Drago darted down the buffalo path to the river, and past the cave, planning to cover the Jap's escape route. He went into the foliage some twenty feet above the cave opening. There, he waited.

Drago heard Akira sprinting towards him. At the last minute, Cpl. Drago emerged from the jungle, blocking Akira's path. Akira did not see his enemy. Drago held his rifle firm and brought up the butt and smashed it into the fleeing soldier's face. As the rush of adrenaline engulfed Drago, he shouted out, "P.T.! P.T. O'Rielly, you son of a bitch!"

There was an instant when Akira tried to stop his forward progress before the butt struck. The force of the stroke dislodged all of Akira's teeth and forced them to his larynx, choking him. The blow snapped his head back, breaking his neck. Akira's brain sent out motor responses to the rest of his body. Although in the throes of death, his feet continued to run. Prancing in air, his head went back, his body somersaulted. He fell, as a cat would out of a tree, on all fours.

Drago, in his fury, drew his knife and thrust it into the dead man, still shouting, "P.T. O'Rielly." Finally, he knelt. His chest heaved; the need for oxygen suppressed all other responses.

He looked at Akira and noticed how small he was. Drago noticed a small satchel the man carried on a string around his neck. He opened the bag, thrust his hand in and felt something familiar.

The Cat's Ass

Major Goto clung to his perch while the river receded. Tatsuo did not appear. Goto cared not, his own destiny was paramount. Loss of other men was insignificant. He planned to set up subversive action until the Emperor's forces returned.

~~~~~~~~~~~~~~~

Sergeants Perlas and Braxton gathered the men around them. Braxton spoke. "I want all of you to form a skirmish line and scour the jungle around the stockade. You should end up back here. There are twelve of you; spread out. You should be far enough away from each other to see only the man to your left or right. Do not lose sight of the man on either side of you. Be as quiet as you can; it's possible we can catch him off-guard. If I hear any one of you bullshitting, you're gonna get it from me. This guy is dangerous. If attacked, kill the son of a bitch."

Perlas was about to join the group when Braxton held him back.

"You and me, we'll follow the river on the north side of camp and wait for the rest to come around. It's possible they'll flush that sucker out, and send him in our direction."

Braxton broke through some brush just as Major Goto's head emerged above the flowing current.

"Looka that cat's ass. He don't know we're here," he said to Perlas.

Braxton moved to the river just as the Japanese major tried to move away. Sgt. Braxton rushed him. The major's eyes scanned the river bed. Goto was vulnerable for just one instant. Then he saw the sergeant coming towards him; he braced one foot on the bank and shot out with the other, catching Braxton under his rib cage. The assault broke three of his ribs. Braxton fell. Goto turned to the river to flee. Before he reached the water, Perlas was on him.

The Battle

Hiroshi ran down the path after Akira. He had a feeling of dread after the shot was fired. If there was more of the enemy, they could have set up an ambush at the cave. He wanted to intercept Akira before he reached their hideout. Drago was inspecting the packet when Hiroshi approached. Seeing Akira lying on the ground, Hiroshi halted, then his anger caused him to shout out, "Aiee, aiee!" He burst forward. Drago, alarmed by the fierceness of the cry, turned his head toward Hiroshi. Hiroshi rammed into the corporal, throwing him down to the river bank. As Drago fell, he released his rifle to free his hands and break his fall. The rifle flew into the river. Drago panicked, and was about to go after it.

Hiroshi noted fear in the Marine's eyes. *This person is in disarray; he is mine. He shall die under my hand.*

He unsheathed Cpl. Paul's bayonet from its scabbard, and darted down to the river bank. Drago looked up just as Hiroshi came at him. The gleaming bayonet caught his attention. In a flash, he thought, *that's an American bayonet he's got. Where did he get it? You crazy shit, that's what you think about? That prick is gonna kill ya!*

Drago raised his arm as the down-thrust of the bayonet sliced his upper arm. Hiroshi pulled the bayonet back, then raised it to strike again. The corporal grabbed his wrist stopping the thrust, and held it fast above Hiroshi's head; his other hand flew out and smashed into the Jap's face. Hiroshi's head snapped back. Hiroshi reached up and grabbed the Marine's throat. Drago's free hand grabbed the wrist at his neck. He tried to get free of the stranglehold Hiroshi had on him. The pressure on his throat cut off his air supply.

Drago knew if he did not loosen the man's hold, he was going to die. In an instant he made a decision to let go of the hand holding the knife so he could bring both his hands to bear on the chokehold. The bayonet shot downward and cut through the corporal's fatigues and into his thigh.

Drago's fist smashed into Hiroshi's face, then with both hands grabbing the Japanese soldier's wrist, he wrenched himself free.

Hiroshi sliced his opponent's thigh to the bone. Drago let go of Hiroshi's wrist, and with great force, slapped his open palms on Hiroshi's ears. Both ear drums were instantly shattered with the effect of an exploding shell. Hiroshi faltered, dazed.

The corporal, realizing his advantage, unsheathed his knife and thrust into Hiroshi below the groin. Hiroshi desperately threw his arms around Drago, as much to hold on as to attack. He hacked at the corporal's back with the bayonet.

Drago tried to push the blade upward, but it would not move. He then grabbed the hilt with both hands. The knife tore upward through Hiroshi's stomach and stopped at his breast bone. Drago removed the blade. Amazingly, Hiroshi kept stabbing the Marine in the back. Enraged, Drago then thrust the knife into the side of the Japanese and drew it across his body, holding the shaft there. Both bodies were fused together, drenched in blood. Hiroshi's blade was imbedded in the Croat's back. Hiroshi, in his final death throes, could not remove it. They stood there, life's blood melding in fusion.

Drago whispered into Hiroshi's dead ear, "Jeremy, Jeremy McVey."

Perlas thought to subdue the major by wrapping his arms about his chest, and immobilize him with a bear hug. Goto's martial arts talent thwarted the sergeant's action; both of his elbows bashed into the sergeant's ribs, forcing him to loosen his hold long enough for the major to thrust his body forward. He was free.

Goto rushed the sergeant. Perlas side stepped. The major went careening into the brush, and somersaulting to an upright position, he faced Perlas. A right cross by the sergeant snapped Goto's head to one side. Perlas jabbed with his left. The major's hand flashed out; with open palm he caught the sergeant's fist. He then twisted his body, bending down on one knee. With his other hand he caught the sergeant at the crook of his elbow and flipped him over into the air. Perlas landed in the river. Goto rushed the stunned Marine and stood over him. With both hands he seized the sergeant's head and pressed his thumbs into the sergeant's eye sockets. Perlas grabbed both the major's wrists, saving his eyes. A stalemate ensued; neither could let go of the other. They growled. Both tried to dislodge the other, using their feet as weapons. The major was winning the battle.

Braxton, in pain, watched them grappling in the river. The patrol had circumvented the stockade and the Marines stood watching the melee. Braxton snatched a rifle from one of the Marines and aimed at the combatants. He remembered the major addressing an inferior in rank, and how the words had affected the Japanese soldier. The soldier became submissive, and bowed his head. Braxton shouted out, from his innards, "Choto! Choto!"

Major Goto turned his head at the command. He looked with dismay at Sergeant Braxton, and Braxton shot him right between the eyes.

Braxton repeated, "Choto" to the now-dead major, adding, "you rat bastard!"

He gave the rifle back to the Marine.

Major Goto's death did not cause much concern; it was inevitable in any case. Col. Kramer and Lt. Warren rationalized that it had saved the hangman a lot of trouble.

Souvenirs & Preservation

Drago reached over his shoulder and pulled Paul's bayonet out of his back, then angrily stabbed Hiroshi with it. The artery in Drago's thigh was severed from Hiroshi's earlier desperate blow. Bleeding from wounds in his back, arm, and thigh, he stood over the men he killed, groaning in pain.

"I will die here if I don't get myself together." He said out loud to the now-dead Hiroshi. He used his knife to cut strips of cloth from his fatigues; twisting the strips together he made a tourniquet and placed it just above the bleeding gash in his thigh.

I gotta move outta here. I have to get help. It's getting dark; I have to get to the road. Jeez, I'm in pain. Dummy, don't waste time, get goin', he reprimanded himself for his hesitation.

The corporal went to the river and searched the water for his rifle. His hand found the sling, and he pulled the rifle out.

He was about to leave when he remembered the satchel and the objects that seemed familiar. The satchel was open; he thrust his hand in and pulled out two gunmetal Marine Corps insignia. The corporal became enraged, knowing the enemy could not possess such items unless those carrying them were dead.

"Souvenirs, ya pricks, souvenirs from the souvenir-hunting Marines from a year past, ya sons a bitches!" he said. He kicked the dead men, then put the emblems in his pocket.

When I get back home I'm gonna find P.T. and Jeremy's people and give one of these to each of them. That's what I'm gonna do.

His wounds drained his strength; he started off with much effort.

I'll find the two ridges and I'll be home. No, no, too hard, follow the river it's got to go to the sea, his mind raced.

Deda's Prediction

Drago took a path that ended about a mile into his trek, leaving him to traverse the river bank. It would be hard to move now, but he had to follow the river. He trudged slowly onward. He stopped after awhile, and pulled out one of the canteens from its sack and drank. Then he poured water on his wounds, and bathed his neck, empting the canteen. He took deep breaths, trying clear his head, then moved on.

Drago was taught that he had to loosen the tourniquet every half hour; it was important to let the blood flow, so that his leg would not die. It was time to loosen it, yet he dared not stop. He went on without adjusting it. The tourniquet was blood-soaked.

His body moved automatically, his mind wandering again. His grandfather came to him.

"*Dete, slushi*, child, listen. It is written that every third generation male shall die in battle. You follow your destiny. There is no escape. I gave you my spirit, you have done well. *Tvoi brat spava na grobye*. Your brothers are buried in the cemetery. *Dobra yeh. Slatka moy deta*, it is good, my sweet child. I watched as you conquered; you hold true to our tradition."

"*Moy Deda*, it was important for me to seek revenge. Yet I do not wish to die."

"*Taka ida Dragomier, moy Hervarti. Chekam tebe.*"

"Don't wait for this Croat; I am not going to the grave. *Deda*, I wish to go home."

The old man faded away. Drago's strength was waning, yet he went on.

One Man's Mission

Nakamura heard the rifle report as he sat in the dugout. Dropping the shrimp trap he was weaving, he reached for the rifle and pocketed the last three shells. The single shot made him wonder if there was more than one person out there.

Could it be Hiroshi? He wondered. *I have told him not to use the rifle; it is only to be used in defense, not as a tool for food. He does not listen. I must take care. It would be odd for a patrol to be coming out after such a storm. Take care, Nakamura,* he cautioned himself.

He left his home. He snaked easily through the reeds and grasses. His pace was slow. He often stopped to listen, but heard nothing. He was too far away to hear the confrontation that was taking place in the subdivision of the Talofofo River. The jungle muted sound.

Sgt. Nakamura cautiously left the jungle for the river path. He came out upriver from the confrontation. It puzzled him, that single report.

What has happened here? Is it my people, or the Americans come in force? Take care Nakamura, take care.

As he approached a curve in the path he crouched, and cautiously peered ahead. There he saw the bodies of Hiroshi and Akira. He froze.

Where are they, the Americans? Is it a trap?

His instincts served him well, so far. He did not move. Any sound could be heard.

The Marines are fierce, but impatient. They easily give themselves away.

Fifteen minutes passed. With no sound or movement, there was no reason to wait any longer. He approached his dead comrades. The Japanese sergeant studied the surroundings and concluded there had been only one other combatant.

Why has one man come on this mission? It is not like them to send one man alone.

He remained at a loss to understand the reason for the destruction of his brothers in arms by this one man.

Surveying the area, he determined that this Marine had stalked his people. He rose and brushed past some vegetation as he followed Drago's shuffling footprints. Blood on leaves; his enemy was wounded. He followed the trail of blood to the river bank.

Taka Ida Dete

Drago smelled the sea. His worn body faltered as he approached the road. On the other side of the road, he heard the soft surf of the Talofofo estuary. The sand glistened in the reflected rays of the setting sun. He thought of the beach that the Seabees constructed near Agana harbor. He did not know that Cpl. Paul's last thoughts were of the same beach.

Yeah, I'm gonna get better and go swimming there, he told himself. *The ocean is like a mirror. You can see the pink coral at its bottom. Maybe some pretty ladies there, maybe Valeriana. I can feel her presence it's her scent. Or maybe Sarah, that would be nice.*

Oh, Christ I hurt, blood on my hand, and in my heart.

The blood around his leg was now cool to the touch; it still dripped down his leg and into his boots. He looked at the sea to his front.

I'll go to the sea and wash away the hurt. The sea will save me.

As he crossed the road, a shot rang out. The bullet passed through Drago's shoulder, a second shot tore into his side. Turning, he faced Sgt. Nakamura. The sergeant held his rifle at his side. Realizing his enemy had not fallen; he raised his rifle and inserted the last cartridge, then brought the weapon up to his shoulder.

Drago's grandfather appeared.

"*Taka ida dete.*" said the apparition.

Drago answered, "That's how it is, *Deda.*"

Drago defiantly put his hand in his pocket and drew out the emblems of the Corps. He opened his hand, showing his trophies to his enemy, then closed his fist.

Sgt. Nakamura could not see what the Marine was showing him, but he bowed ever so slightly, just the slightest tilting of his head forward in recognition of the warrior facing him. He set his sights and fired, then turned towards the jungle and vanished.

The bullet entered Drago's lung just above his heart. The corporal fell forward.

His thoughts were of his grandfather. He said, *Taka ida Deda.*

Comfort in Death

Gunnery Sergeant Killian sped his Jeep along the sea highway. His visit to the outer village he adopted had been fruitful. Three ham quarters rested in the rear seat. His lady friend, as he called her, was quite cooperative; it was a good trip.

He was slightly woozy from the vodka he had consumed on his visit. He drank heavily, but did not get drunk. His speech was slurred, which left him unable to spew the profane expletives he would have had he been sober. He hummed a tune. It was all right to do so as long as he was alone; not manly otherwise. The manly thing was important to him.

As he sped around a curve, he saw a body in the road in front of his careening Jeep. He slammed on the brakes; the Jeep swerved towards the sea. Two wheels left the road. He shuddered, remembering the Jeep as a lethal thing, being prone to accidents, killing more men than he could count. Leaning his body to the off-wheel side, he righted the vehicle. He stopped.

"Who the hell is that, fer Christ sakes? Oh, yeah, some dumbass drunken Marine lying there, stupid shit!"

He approached the corporal.

Damn if I don't know that rascal. That's the piss-ant that held me up at the gate when I went to visit Perlas and Braxton at the N.C.O. club. Yeah, he's from the Ninth Triple A outfit. Dumb shit layin' there.

As he came close to the prone body, he realized Drago's condition was dire. He went down on one knee and immediately surveyed the area.

Sons a bitches are still out there! How did this kid get way out here? Jesus Christ, he's bleedin' all over! What the fuck's happened here?

The wounds were so obvious and many, the sergeant squirmed at the sight of them. He felt for the boy's pulse. It was ever so slight.

The corporal opened his eyes. He held up one hand with the trophies and offered them to the gunny.

"Jesus kid, we gotta get you outta here."

Drago tried to speak; the fear of his coming death overwhelmed him. His speech slurred as he addressed the gunny. "No, no, my *Deda* told me."

The sergeant did not understand what Drago said, but he smiled at him as though he did. Drago wished Gunnery Sergeant Killian would take the gifts he offered. He held them tight for fear of losing them. The Gunny knew there was nothing he could do for the corporal.

"All right, you're gonna be all right; the old gunner is gonna take care of you."

He sat next to Drago and put the Marine's head on his thigh, and patted him on the shoulder.

"Don't ya worry son, the gunny's here, he's gonna watch over you."

As he sat waiting for the boy to die, his thoughts went back to the incident at the gate of the antiaircraft battalion. Drago was firm, and told the gunny not to put his Jeep in gear before he called the N.C.O. club.

"Screw you, ya little shit! You piss-ant, you can't stop me from goin' in ta see my friends, I'm goin' in," he railed at the corporal.

"Don't do it gunny; don't move the Jeep. I have to call in first."

The gunny pressed down on the clutch pedal and threw it in gear. Before he could release the clutch, Drago pulled out the pistol from its holster and set it on the lip of the window in the gatehouse. Then he picked up the phone and called in.

"I got a sergeant out here says he's your guest."

Perlas, on the other end of the phone, told Drago, "It's okay; let him in."

Drago holstered the pistol and flagged in the Jeep.

The gunny burst into the club, cursing.

"That piss-ant better not get in my way again. If he does, I'm gonna pound him into the ground. He pulled that fuckin' pistol on me, right there, the little shit."

Perlas, Braxton, and the battalion sergeant major were sitting around a card table; they all laughed so hard the room shook.

Braxton then related the various incidents that put Drago in high esteem in their eyes: the P.O.W. stockade and Henry James, Callahan sleeping on post, the story of the pistol-wielding orderly, his confrontation with the lieutenant; all were embellished. The tales did not appease the furious gunnery sergeant. All through the card game he would not let it rest, yet he left that evening convinced that the Corps would hold up as long as they had men with guts like Cpl. Stoyon.

Drago Stoyon died in his arms. He picked him up, and with great care laid him down in the back seat of the Jeep. He moved off slowly; there was no rush now. Even in death, the sergeant wished the boy comfort.

"Shit," he said, and pinched his eyes with thumb and index finger, drawing away the moisture that flooded them.

The Sergeants

Gunnery Sergeant Killian pulled into the Triple-A battalion and carried Cpl. Stoyon into the N.C.O. club. He had the boy draped over his shoulder. He laid him down at a card table where Perlas and Braxton sat. After a few moments of stunned silence, Braxton was the first to speak. "What a fuckin' loss! We knew what he was up to, but just couldn't stop him." The gunny looked confused by the statement.

The two sergeants explained Drago's mission to Killian.

The gunny pried open the corporal's hand, which still held the Marine Corps emblems.

"Here, he had these in his hand. He mumbled something, I couldn't get it. He was alive when I got there. Then he died."

Perlas went to the body and took the trophies from the corporal's hand.

"I know what they're for. I'll take care of them," said Perlas.

It was late; they left the body where it lay, and each went his separate way.

Sgt. Braxton's quarters were in the same Quonset as Cpl. Stoyon; he had to pass through Stoyon's to get to his own billet. On a shelf above the Croat's bunk stood a huge book. It was the *Blue Jackets Manual* that he left the corporal awhile back, a gift from one Marine to another.

Sergeant Braxton stopped and gazed at the manual, he then sat on Drago's bunk.

I wonder what we should get together to send home with him? He brushed his hand on the blanket to straighten it. *All these years, he thought, and all the good men gone. I wonder how they could have made life better for us all if they had lived. The kid had the brains, and the guts to be an exemplary Marine. Christ, what a shame.*

His thoughts went back to the meeting with Perlas when they both had been preparing the sergeant's test. They discussed Drago's chances of besting the other corporals. Taking the test for sergeant did not guarantee him receiving the warrant. Points were given for combat time and for time in a war zone. Three other corporals had amassed enough points to pass Stoyon; Perlas and Braxton wanted one of the warrants to go to Drago. A decision was made by the two sergeants to give Stoyon an edge. They could not agree on how it could be done.

"I'll take care of it," said Braxton. He left and took the book with him. Perlas asked no questions, and went on his way

That evening, the corporal, lying in his bunk, mulled over the situation. He realized his position, knowing it was quite improbable that he could fare well enough to receive the promotion. The door opened and Braxton came in. He addressed Drago. "Read the black print," he said, and dropped the book on Drago's stomach. The sergeant didn't miss a step as he exited to his quarters on the other side of the Quonset.

The corporal did not sleep that night. Bleary-eyed, he took the test the next day. The black print prevailed. He passed the fifty question test, missing only one. His score of 98 helped him rise above the other corporals that Perlas and Braxton thought unworthy: "true pricks" in Braxton's eyes.

He won't need this anymore, god damn shame. Braxton took the book off the shelf, and walked off with it under his arm.

Sgt. Perlas laid the emblems on a table next to his bunk. In the morning he would send them to the families of P.T. and Jeremy. He would not send a note with them; he hoped they would understand the reason for the gesture.

The Legion

Juarez's tour was up; he finished his 24 months overseas. As a regular Marine, he was rewarded with a furlough of sixty days; it came as Drago's body was to be sent home. He would accompany the body of Cpl. Stoyon to his home in Pennsylvania and see that the funeral service was militarily correct and performed with due respect. Then he would go home.

He sat on the train as it rumbled towards its destination, and remembered a conversation he had with the Croat. It was one of those days when you just sat by the side of the road, and didn't say much. They were both at ease, Stoyon resting on the trunk of a tree, Juarez sitting on a rock, pitching stones. Drago smoked. Drago was the first to speak.

"Ya know, Juarez, it's been three years now, and it ain't been bad. It wasn't as tough as I thought it would be."

"What's that?" inquired Juarez.

"Bein' in the Corps. So far we got through it all right. What do you think?"

"It ain't as bad as they said it was gonna be," Juarez agreed, and, tired of sitting, got off the rock.

"Not much could be tougher than my old man," Drago said.

Juarez did not respond, but thought about the tough neighborhood of his youth.

Drago thought a moment, and then said, "What do you think about the French Foreign Legion?"

Juarez beamed, an unfamiliar set of white teeth gleamed. Juarez hardly ever smiled.

"Yeah, that would be a hoot," Juarez slapped his knee.

"They're supposed to be a tough bunch a bastards," said Drago, "What say we make a pact? When we finish our four years in the Corps, we somehow get together and join the Foreign Legion."

"Yeah, said the Aztec corporal. "We could see Africa, France. Jesus, what a thought."

"Okay," said Drago, and extended his hand to Juarez. Juarez grasped it and shook it hard.

"On your mother's heart, I promise. Say it," Juarez dared the Croat.

"On my mother's heart," Drago said.

They both laughed heartily.

Tom's Friend

The Guinea from Brooklyn ran into the mess hall and found Tom sitting with the college boys and the newly warranted Sgt. Flint.

"Didja hear about the Croat? Did ya hear what he did?"

"Yeah, yeah," said Tom. "We heard from Callahan, don't know where he got his information from. Besides he ain't a Croat. What the fuck's a Croat? He's a Hunky, a Hungarian, or something like that," Tom lashed out.

"Yeah, the way I heard it he killed a lot of Japs, six Japs, before they got him. That's what I heard." The Brooklyn boy sulked.

"Who told you six Japs, ya dumb ass. Perlas thinks it's two."

"Well, that's what I heard," said the Guinea from Brooklyn, raising his voice.

The Syrian looked up from his meal, glaring at the rest.

"I don't believe a word of it. He went out and got killed. That's all we know. He wasn't much anyway."

Tom got up. He wished to be away. If he stayed any longer, he probably would have whacked the Syrian with his mess tray.

"Just goes ta show ya," said Tom. "You turds don't know your ass from a hole in the ground. That kid had the balls to go in there and even out the score with those scumbags. Shit!"

He wheeled about to leave the mess hall.

"Who else would have done it?" Tom asked them. "Not me, sure as shit, none of you would have. Perlas and Braxton know. He was some Marine, that kid. Yes, sir, I knew him. That makes me proud." He went out.

Two fresh Marines were passing by. He approached them.

"Hey there, what have we here, recruits? We got some raisin jack, a barrel of it other side of the mess hall. All ya gotta do is dip a cup in, skim off the top and pull it out."

The two Marines halted and surveyed Tom. Tom raised the cup he carried, and gave the new people his fatboy smile.

"Let's go," he said. "I gotta make a toast to a friend of mine."

They walked off together.

About the Author

Gene Rackovitch entered the Marine Corps in 1944. In March of 1945, Mr. Rackovitch was attached to C Company, 1ˢᵗ Battalion, 23ʳᵈ Marines, 4ᵗʰ Marine Division. At the end of the Second World War, he was sent to Guam. He was stationed there for eighteen months. It was there that he amassed the material  for *Marines and Renegades*. His previous collections of short stories of the Corps have been highly praised by his comrades in arms, and his first novel, *Zivo*, received critical acclaim from publications such as *Writer's Digest*.

He is a father and a grandfather, and has been married for fifty years. Upon retiring after twenty years driving a milk truck in New York City, he started a jewelry business serving the tourist areas along the east coast from Maine to Key West.

Mr. Rackovitch's guiding philosophy is that 'life is an adventure not only for the celebrated but for each and every one of us.'

Made in the USA
Charleston, SC
15 January 2011